Diverted Heart

Beth Ann Stifflemire

Published by Waldorf Publishing

2140 Hall Johnson Road
#102-345
Grapevine, Texas 76051
www.WaldorfPublishing.com

Diverted Heart
ISBN: 9781942574323
Library of Congress Control Number: 2014922828

Foreword by: Lori Ryan
New York Times Bestselling Author of The Sutton
Capital Series

Mistakes are a part of being human. Appreciate your mistakes for what they are: precious life lessons that can only be learned the hard way. Unless it's a fatal mistake, which, at least, others can learn from. Al Franken, "Oh, the Things I Know", 2002

How many of us wouldn't give anything to have the United States Postal Service finally perfect the science of time travel mail? To be able to mail a letter to our teenage selves, our twenty-year-old selves, even to our young-married-couple selves, and warn of mistakes. How many of us wouldn't give anything to know it's time to say one final *I love you* or *you matter to me* to a loved one? Or to have the certainty of knowing this is *the one*.

In *Diverted Heart*, Beth Ann Stifflemire catches her characters in that moment of time when we leave behind the confusion and uncertainty of high school and embark on the terrifying bewilderment of college life. The main character, Taylor, wants desperately for her high school love for Eric to endure while at the same time struggling with the fact that life is pulling them further apart. And when love between Taylor and another man begins to grow, despite all her efforts to fight her feelings, all three find themselves headed for a result that can only lead to pain for at least one, if not more, of the players.

Stifflemire quickly draws her readers into that wonderful world that exists between childhood and adulthood, with characters you'll root for and cry for and an ending that is hard-won and bittersweet. I hope you enjoy *Diverted Heart* and the journey and characters that make up its pages as much as I did.

Dedication

Hank, thank you for showing me unconditional love and support and inspiring me each and every day. You are my rock! And to Grandma and Grandpa, thank you for allowing me to stay with you all those summers growing up at the farm. Little did I know that it would be the inspirational setting for *Diverted Heart*.

CHAPTER ONE: MOVING DAY

"Come on, Judge!" The eager chocolate Labrador bolts from the back gate, barking in between hops. I clip the red leash to his black collar just in time. He pulls me with him, running at mach speed to the street. "Wait, Judge." He halts only a moment then resumes pulling me until I break into a jog.

It's moving day, and this will be our final run through my childhood neighborhood. Judge stays at my side as I pick up speed. A long-distance runner in high school, this has been a part of my daily routine for the last four years but now it's therapeutic. The unknown of the summer ahead is a constant thought. Running allows a brief escape from the what-ifs cluttering my brain.

Eric called just before my run, which has also become a daily routine in recent weeks, since he left to play football at Kansas State. The first day he left was strange and lonesome. I cried, initially because I missed him. Now

7

when I cry, it's because I'm leaving the only home I remember. A mixture of emotions tugs at my heart as I close a chapter of my youth today.

The well-established, upper middle-class Hunter's Creek Village neighborhood in Houston reminds me of a picturesque scene one might see in a movie. I glance at each home while I run, paying extra attention to them. They transition between big, white plantation-style homes with large columns, to red brick homes with ornate wood detailing at the roof lines and shutters. The street is lined with giant pine trees that leave a layer of pine needles on the black asphalt.

Nicky's repeated "You'll have such a great time when you go to A&M in the fall!" plays over in my mind once again. She's said it to the point I would scream if I heard it again, yet I know she means well. She may not be my birth mother, but she certainly loves me like her own, and is trying to help.

I stop at the street corner, adjust my iPod ear buds blaring Incubus's *Dig* and check my stopwatch. Forty-five minutes since I set the timer—time to head back.

Judge never wavers from his pace, keeping up with me the entire run. I remove his leash when we arrive back at the driveway and walk with him to the gate—
one last time.

"Good boy, Judge. You did so good." Leaning over, I kiss his head, fighting the urge to cry. He licks my sweaty cheek then heads towards his water bowl on the back porch. I shut the wooden gate.

The movers have arrived, and boxes are exiting the house every other minute. With a heavy heart, I return inside, take a quick shower, slide into a pair of denim shorts and a baby blue tank top then walk back into my room. The movers haven't attacked it yet. I stare at the blank walls and filled boxes piled everywhere then locate my cell phone. A text message is showing… just what I need right now:

Love you babe. This is just temporary.

I sigh, imagining his voice speaking the words aloud instead of having to read them in an informal text as a flashback floods my mind. Our last night together:

"God, I'm going to miss you."

He brushed away the tears cascading from my eyes with his strong thumbs then cupped my damp face in his warm hands.

"It won't be easy for me either, but we'll make it work. I want you even from hundreds of miles away."

I forced a slow breath to avoid further tears. Eric placed his lips, deep with want onto mine, kissing me with intent fervor. I wanted more of him, all of him. He pulled me closer into his sturdy arms.

***

"Taylor?" I hear Nicky's voice from downstairs, drawing me back to the present. My mind is hazy. "Taylor?" I hear my name once more.

I move to the doorway and yell back down to her. "Yes?"

"Your room ready?" I walk to the top of the stairs and see her below, near the front door. Her sharply-angled blonde bob is tucked behind one ear, the other side covering her cheek.

"Almost, Mom."

"The movers are ready as soon as you are, Taylor."

"Okay, I'm on it." I grin for Nicky's sake and return to the bedroom, forcing myself to pack the remaining boxes.

A half hour later I'm finished, with a purse and overnight bag draped over my shoulders. I close my eyes a brief moment, remembering all of the things that happened in this space… studying for tests, getting ready for track meets… kissing Eric, second base, third base. My mind is inundated with images that flash in rapid-fire film-like form. Opening my eyes, I twirl a piece of my long dark hair with my fingers and choose not to turn back. I'd rather remember it full of furniture and teeming with life. Releasing the lock of hair, I close the door with one hand behind me and smile as I remember the good times and make my final stroll downstairs.

"Go for a run earlier?" Dad asks, walking through the bare-walled living room, a box under his arm.

"Yeah, I wanted to see it all one last time."

"Well, you'll be able to run to your heart's content in the country, too, you know. Judge would love that."

"Don't know; he'll have so much freedom to roam around the place." My stomach twists in knots, thinking about our new home just hours away.

"Oh, don't be silly. Running with you is one of his favorite things." Dad looks at me with sincerity in his dark eyes.

I stare back at him, my eyes a reflection of his, the only trait we share. Everything else biological is from my mother. At least what I can tell from old pictures.

"Whose favorite things?" Pacey barrels through the room, tossing a baseball into a catcher's mitt.

He has a backpack over his puny ten-year-old shoulders. He's been experimenting with hair gel again, and little spikes peak on his blond head.

"It's nothing, Pacey."

"Whatever." He continues throwing the ball into the catcher's mitt and runs out the front door.

I'm not far behind, heading for my nearly-new Mustang, a very welcomed graduation present from Dad and Nicky; perhaps a Band-Aid effort on their behalf to soften the blow of moving to the sticks. No matter the reason, I'm not complaining. Opening the passenger door, I place my bag and purse neatly on the leather seat.

Nicky emerges from the house in a cream tunic and jeans as I close the Mustang's door. She has paintings beneath each arm. Painting is her passion. Therefore, it's no surprise when she delicately nestles the canvases in the back of her Escalade. Art is one of the earliest memories I have of Nicky. She used to set up a little painting area on an easel next to her, and I'd paint along with her for hours as a child. She was so patient with me, just as she's been patient with my crazed, post-teenage mood swings lately as a result of all the recent changes.

"We should be ready to pull out of here within the hour." Nicky smiles over at me.

"Alright, Mom," I reply, glancing back at her.

***

We've been on the road an hour and a half. The pine trees had thinned into oaks and rural landscapes on the busy I-10 highway after departing Katy, the last big city on the edge of Houston. With the city now far in the rearview mirror, cars zoom around our motorcade, which consists of Dad in his practically brand-new Chevy pickup, Nicky and Pacey in her Escalade, me in the Mustang, and the packed moving truck behind us all. The first sign appears for Schulenburg: 10 miles, I read through my gold rim aviator sunglasses. My car stereo is blaring Mutemath through the speakers, assisting in my escape of the unwelcome surroundings about to come to fruition. My cell phone buzzes in the seat next to me, Eric's familiar ring of Bob Marley's *Could This Be Love* barely audible with the music blaring. I turn the radio down.

13

"Hello?" I answer.

"How's my girl?" Eric's voice soothes me.

"Hmm," I let out a sigh, "About to pull into my new digs. Shouldn't be much longer."

"I know it's a weird day, Taylor. Hang in there, babe."

"Why do I miss you so much?" I grip the steering wheel so tightly my knuckles turn white with my non-phone-holding hand. It's a source of stress release.

"Same reason I miss you so much. I love you, Taylor."

I breathe long and hard, casting a brief silence on the line.

"When do you start training?" I decide to change the subject.

"Soon. Trying to work out every day now, plus getting to know the campus better. It's different. I think you'll be happy when you go to A&M in the fall. It's nice to meet people. Although they're pretty scarce right now, a few are here for summer session."

"I'd take school over my current option. I should've listened to my dad and started classes this summer instead of the fall. I clearly wasn't thinking."

"Relax, Taylor, enjoy the summer. It will be all-out crazy when you get to campus in a few months."

The onset of what seems like depression riddles my mind when Eric utters *"months"*. Crap, I don't want to be here that long, and I haven't even gotten to *here* yet. My *here* is full of angst, and I feel tears loom as I clear my throat.

"I know you're about to cry; you're clearing your throat—telltale sign. Please don't."

I sigh and shake my head to rid the pressing tears as I see our entourage make an exit off the highway.

"Listen, I better go; we're getting off the highway and I don't really know where we're headed from here. Call you later?"

"I'll be waiting for the call. Love you."

"You, too." I smile and hang-up.

***

It's been nearly twenty minutes since we left I-10 and passed downtown Schulenburg, which appeared to be a one-street town, if that. We meander down rural road upon rural road, finally turning onto a red dirt road. *Oh lovely.* I've never been to this place, farm, whatever you want to call it, so I have no clue what I'm looking for.

Eventually, Dad slows down in the Chevy at the front of our moving train, and turns into a rickety gate that's been left open. There's a mailbox out front, displaying the numbers 215. I see a very old-looking white farmhouse in the distance. The paint flaking from its outward exterior can be observed from more than a quarter mile down the drive.

Dad hasn't said much about the condition of the house, but it's obviously in need of some repair. I suppose he and Nicky aren't hugely concerned with it, since they intend to build their *dream house* come fall. The plans for the construction are already drawn up and ready to rock-n-roll. The house in Houston sold quickly. I'd overheard them discussing taking their time, finalizing loans, finding contractors, etcetera, so the actual building of the new house won't be while I'm here.

Upon closer approach, the farmhouse's disheveled condition is clear; green shutters also peeling of paint, a scattering of missing roof shingles, and a yard in serious need of some weed-pulling.

I park the car a good distance from the house, assuming the movers will need close proximity. I don't want my beautiful Mustang in the line of fire.

Get your big-girl face on, Taylor.

I look in the rearview mirror at my chocolate eyes staring back at me, and coerce a smile for the sake of my family. Climbing out of the car, I take a slow 360-degree view of the surroundings. *Wow, there is nothing out here.* I see fields of tall grass, barbed-wire fences, giant ancient-looking oaks, and cattle sprinkled throughout the horizon in various fields. About to complete my scan, I take notice of a large, red barn to one side of the house, a good distance away. It's at least a ten-minute walk I gauge. The only other buildings to be seen are a few rooftops, miles away. *Depressing. Two months to freedom* repeats through my brain.

"Taylor!" I hear my name yelled. "What do you think?" Dad waves over at me, gesturing towards the countryside.

I shrug my shoulders, giving him a silent answer. Lugging my overnight bag and purse out of the car, I sling them over my shoulder and make way toward the house. Not Houston by far; such an old house, not anything I'm accustomed to. *Welcome to my temporary summer hell.* The only momentary happiness is my beautiful Judge running towards me, tail wagging and happy to see me.

CHAPTER TWO: HANDSOME STRANGER

"So, what's it like?" Eric begins the grand inquiry on our evening phone call.

"Old, old, and older. The floors are worn with scuffs, it smells musty, and the windows have this weird beveled look to them."

"Wow, it does sound old," Eric responds.

I had no warning about just how old the place really is. It had been owned by my great uncle, Charlie Sabian. I hardly remember meeting the man, though I know I had. I was very young, maybe five or six. We were at a family reunion, and he sat at a table with a bunch of other old men, consumed in a game of dominos. I can't shake the memory of his enormous ears and nose, almost like a real-life caricature. Dad said he'd never married, was born here and died here. *Creepy.*

"Yeah, place looks like it's hardly been touched since the old man passed." I pull the edge of the curtain back in my upstairs bedroom and see only pitch-black darkness.

"Do you have any ideas of stuff to do around there?" *Really, Eric?*

"Ha. Yeah, I'll just hit up the Starbucks around the corner and then go shopping at the mall," I reply with disdain. "Place is in the middle of nowhere, Eric. A serial killer could hack us to pieces and no one would find us for days."

"You'll figure something out, Taylor. Don't get down in the dumps."

We both pause and a brief, awkward silence ensues as if we're each unsure of what to talk about.

"Well, I love you if it makes any difference." I can sense Eric's smile through the phone.

"Thanks, babe. Love you, too."

***

As the evening wears on, I detect the commotion around the house quieting. Slowly, the lights from downstairs turn off one by one, until the entire house is dark and still. The room I settled into is one of two upstairs. Pacey commandeered the other bedroom, which was slightly larger. I let him have first dibs, knowing I would *thankfully* not be here for the long haul.

The smell of mothballs lingers, old wood slats line the ceiling and, through the window, the brightest stars I've ever laid eyes on cast a bright glow into the small bedroom.

I want to tinker on the laptop I'd recently received as a graduation present, but remember Dad saying it'd be a few days before the satellite Internet could be set up. *Figures.* Instead, I toy with ideas in my head of anything I can do to maintain my sanity the rest of the summer. What to do, what to do? Run? That would use up an hour. Read? Maybe a little, but I'll be doing more reading than I will ever want when fall semester commences. Meet people? Ha, where? I could take up painting again, I suppose. I had never thought myself to be good—not nearly as gifted as Nicky—but it's relaxing and time-consuming.

"Ugh." I pull a pillow over my head and fall flat onto the bed. It creaks as I collapse into it and my dark waves cascade around me. Desperate to transport myself into another world, I collect the iPod on the bedside table and stick the ear buds in my ears. I wrap my arms around Eric's oversized football jersey. It's the only thing I'm wearing over my panties, and smells like him, though less and less with each wear. I want him here now.

I stare out at the stars through the window, feeling my breathing slow, and pray aloud, "Please help this summer go by quickly. Whatever I'm supposed to take away from this, *please* make it worth my while… something. Anything."

I tuck myself into a ball, and let Cold Play's music gently lull me to sleep.

***

Waking the next morning, I yearn for a thorough run to release my tensed emotions. I change into a pair of tight black running shorts with a hot pink sports bra, and pull on a pair of socks, hiding my fuchsia painted toenails. After careening down the ancient, steep stairs to the kitchen for a quick bite to eat, I see Nicky pouring herself a cup of coffee while Dad sits at the table, eating a bagel.

"What's up, pup?" Dad smiles. He's called me *pup* since I was little, which I've found both annoying and sweet as the years have passed.

"Think I'm going to run and explore a little."

"Plenty of room to run out here, for sure."

"Just be careful, and take Judge with you, would you?"

"Wouldn't want to go without him."

"Want some toast or a bagel?" Nicky offers.

"Toast sounds good." I grab an already-toasted piece from the plate on the table, slap some peanut butter on it, and devour it. I immediately follow that with a glass of water to help the heavy peanut butter down my throat and hydrate for the run. Now energized with breakfast, I brush my teeth quickly in the bathroom and pile my hair into a makeshift bun on top of my head.

After locating Judge's leash set on a half-opened box in the tight living area, I stroll out the old, rusted screen door, once again taking in the vast countryside stretched in all directions.

"Judge." The lounging dog pops up from a nap on the front porch, tongue displayed and tail wagging as he approaches. After hooking the leash to his collar, I begin a slow walk to the front of the property, down the dirt road, pausing to intermittently stretch one leg and then the other as I decide which direction tickles my fancy. After reaching the open gate at the property entrance, I pick the route appearing to be more thickly wooded with enormous oaks and hackberry trees, and take off.

I'm in my happy place, the only happy place that is familiar to me right now. Running is like freedom, and such an adrenaline release. After jogging to the end of the initial country road, I am again tasked with choosing a direction. On the horizon is an enormous house of cream-colored rock, trees lining the length of the drive, and it piques my interest.

"Come on, Judge." I tug him gently in the direction I'm set on, and he follows. Running past the enormous house, I can't help but take in the beautifully landscaped property and painted white fencing that encompasses it. I imagine the owners are in for a bit of competition, based on what Nicky and Dad have in mind for their new home. Their house plans appeared a bit different from this one, more plantation-like, but I'd only glanced at them briefly, having little interest. I knew I'd rarely—if ever—live there. Yet, even after a brief view, the sizes of the houses seem comparable.

The large house leaving my line of sight, I let my real running legs kick in and it's off to the races, Judge at my side. After running as far as I feel comfortable, I begin to navigate my way back home. *If that's what you'd call it.*

Sweat drips from my hair, even up in its makeshift bun, and my skin glistens in the morning sun from the layer of perspiration that's built up. The vitamin D soaking into my olive skin is welcomed, and will no doubt turn my skin a shade darker. Tanning is never a problem, and during summer's shorts-wearing season, I am always grateful for it, glad I don't have to deal with the over-the-counter self-tanning crap.

This has been, by far, the quietest run I've ever been on. I had left my iPod at the house to pay closer attention to where I am going, and the stillness that surrounds me is a strange sort of quiet that seems to only exist in this new, unfamiliar and isolated countryside. The familiar hustle and bustle of busy cars and honking horns from Houston is long gone. The old farmhouse comes into sight, and I slow my stride.

Against the quiet that's consumed the entire run, a loud rumble a short distance away instantly distracts me. Hearing the annoyingly loud noise quickly approach, I step to the roadside just as a large, lifted white pickup truck flies past, sending dust in every direction. *What the hell?* I cough as the dust lifts, ready to shoot a middle finger into the air and choose a few colorful words for whatever jackass has just passed, when the truck comes to a halt with lit-up brake lights. *Oh hell. This isn't good.* Abduction comes to mind as the truck slowly backs up in my direction. Should I run? Would Judge attack if I needed him to? My heart is beating gigantic palpitations in my chest.

The truck slows to a stop so the tinted window of the driver's side is even with me, then rolls down, emitting the sound of some twangy country song—*Silver Wings* I think—that's playing on the radio. The driver is now visible, and I am startled by an unexpectedly good-looking guy, slightly older than me, by the looks of him. He has a wide, all-pristine-teeth grin, dark blond, yet sun-kissed, hair cut short but a bit unruly, and rich, dark eyes with flecks of hazel in them.

"Hi there, pretty lady," the stranger speaks with a rugged voice and a sultry drawl.

I don't know whether to read him the riot act for his crazy, asinine driving, or stare in awe at his surprisingly handsome features. I decide on the smartass route.

"What the hell is your basic malfunction? You could've creamed me if I hadn't heard you coming." Judge sits calmly at my side, but perks up his ears with the sudden raise in my voice.

"Whoa, sassy." He lifts his hands above his head as if under arrest. "I apologize, young lady. It's not everyday people decide to take a walk on these country back roads."

He returns his hands to the steering wheel. I quickly glance over the vehicle, noticing a large, black, duffel-like bag in the back of the truck. It makes me nervous.

"What is that?" I point at the black bag peeking out of the bed of the truck.

"What?" He looks surprised. "Why don't we just start with, Hi, my name is Maxwell Bara, Max to most. Yours?"

I feel slightly—*slightly*—bad for my ill manners, so I momentarily reciprocate. "Taylor." I strive to give away no hint of emotion, feeling my lips struggle to hold a hard line and not shift into a smile.

"Oh, she has a name…Taylor. Beautiful name." He grins, again revealing his salacious smile.

"Boy, you come on strong, don't you, Maxwell?" I try hard to hold my ground.

"Like I said, most people call me Max, but Maxwell works, too." He presses his lips together. I can see he's not accustomed to his full name, and it beckons my devious side.

"Well, *Maxwell*, would you like to answer my question?" I point again to the back of the truck.

"Oh, the bag again." He glances back at it and then to me, and offers a mischievous grin. "That's where I hide the bodies," he half laughs, half acts serious.

"Huh?" I don't know how to take his answer, shifting my attention once again to Judge. "Well, this is my dog, Judge. He's very protective, so you may want to steer clear." I, of course, announce this as Judge rolls over on the ground to have his belly rubbed. *Lovely timing, Judge.*

"Uh huh….terrifying. But he's a good-looking dog anyway." Max props himself up slightly to see Judge out of the passenger window. After taking a gander at my dog's antics, his eyes travel the length of my body before meeting mine. *Real slick, dude.* "I live up the way. The white house, just up the road here." He points back the way he'd come.

"I saw it when I was running. Nice place." I've slightly relaxed, knowing he lives in the enormous house. The serial killer stigma I initially attached to the new stranger diminishes. Surely a handsome guy who lives in a nice house wouldn't hack me to pieces—I think.

"Where did you drop out of the sky from?" He laughs.

"Well…" I ruminate on whether I want to actually tell this insanely handsome stranger where I live, and then give in to temptation. "Here." I motion back at the old farmhouse.

"So, you moved into the old Sabian place. Glad someone finally did. Shame to see it empty these last few months."

"Uh huh. Well, I'm not exactly thrilled about it." I roll my eyes. "And it's not mine. It's my parents'."

"City girl? Just guessing." He laughs as I nod my head obnoxiously up and down. "Well, *city girl,* when you get bored enough, which I'm sure you're beyond already, I'm right up the road." He winks.

This is where I decide to interject the *I have a boyfriend* spiel, but I don't have the chance, as he continues too quickly.

"I've got to get on down the road. Got somewhere I need to be." He offers a sinful smile and hooded eyes. "Got to get rid of that body in the back, but it just made my day makin' your acquaintance… Taylor." His grin grows to nearly bursting at the seams, followed by a swift wave.

The window rolls up and he takes off down the dirt road, leaving me speechless at his obviously flirtatious introduction, and still pissed at his reckless driving. Judge breaks my trance, licking at my knee.

"Well, Judge, not sure what that was all about." Ungluing myself from the spot I've been planted in since the truck stopped, I steer Judge back towards the ancient farmhouse. "Come on, Judge." He follows, and I continue as if he understands. "Thanks for the unbelievably protective, scary dog routine you just demonstrated," I giggle slightly. *It was sort of funny.*

Unruly sun-kissed hair and hazel eyes cloud my thoughts, and then somewhere during the remaining distance home, Eric resurfaces after the muffled haze of the morning's events begin to lapse.

CHAPTER THREE: FIND AN ESCAPE

I can't stay cooped up in the house, especially with no Internet and no one to speak with but my family. Dad won't be starting at the clinic for another week, and is busy with a zillion fix-it projects around the old house —inside and out—though I don't understand why he bothers, with the new home on the horizon. Nicky has already begun painting country landscapes on the front porch, and Pacey runs incessantly outside, in infinite freedom, tossing that damn ball in his catcher's mitt.

That morning had, I assumed, allotted to the largest excitement of the day. With a boyfriend on my brain, I decide to ignore the strange encounter with Max completely, not even informing Dad or Nicky about the neighbor I'd met. Who'd have thought, of the most desolate existence and lack of neighbors possible, that Mr. Handsome'R'Us lives at the only house I can make out for miles. Someone my age does sound appealing, though. *You have a boyfriend, Taylor. Hanging out with a guy, the only guy for miles….not a good idea.*

"Stop it!" I can't contain myself, and yell aloud.

Exploring the property is just about the only other thing I can think to do for the day to rid myself of these unexpected thoughts. I take off from the house towards the old red barn I saw when we first arrived. Judge appears, his chocolate lab hips swinging side-to-side. I smile down at him. He licks at my leg once, and more than ever I appreciate his loyalty in a place where I feel so lonely.

The barn is a good distance from the house, and I pass two fields on the dirt path along the way. As I approach, I notice that the barn's paint is more of a tangerine color from sun-fading. A few boards are missing, and others show obvious rot, but it's a large building and would require a good deal of care to maintain. I head for the latched door and lift it slowly. It offers a spooky creak as it swings open. What appears before me is like stepping back in time. Old leather straps and ring-like objects dangle from nails on the wall, a very old tractor sits idly under layers of dust and soot, and hay is stacked neatly along one entire side of the enormous structure.

Judge peeks inside, sniffs the ground, and then commences a full-out scent analysis of every crook and crevice in the space. I take in the smell of must and hay and circle once, slowly. It's no mall, for sure, but it could make a great escape from the house if needed. I sit on a lone bale of hay and close my eyes tightly, taking a deep breath of barn air.

Eric's beautiful eyes invade my thoughts, taking me back to the memory of our first date my junior year. I could hardly peel my gaze away from those beautiful blue eyes, and I think I fell for him even then. Yes, we're young. Yes, this is the first time I've been in love. So, where will our love really go? I wish I knew, but really, I just know I don't want to lose our connection. Unfortunately, distance, time, and school will all compete with it. What I know for certain now is that I miss him. I miss him so much I ache. I shake my head, hoping to stop the onslaught of tears I feel coming on, and see a rickety wooden ladder leading to the loft. I approach it and reach out to wiggle it a bit, testing its sturdiness.

Though old, it's in relatively fair shape, so I brace myself with a hand on each side and begin to climb. I hear

Judge whine once, and glance back to see him sitting, with a worried look in his eyes.

"It's okay, Judge." I turn and resume the climb.

After about twelve rungs, I reach the top. There isn't much to see, just a very small window-like door dangling open. I carefully place my feet on the old loft's wooden boards and walk across, having to duck in a few places to avoid hitting the rafters. Reaching the cracked opening, I push it completely open and hear it bang against the outside of the barn. I am completely taken aback by what I see.

The countryside is spread across my view like a beautiful painting. An enormous, picturesque pond sits a good walk away; moss-covered oaks, with whimsical limbs hanging low to the ground, lining its banks. The moss sways in the hot summer breeze and activates ripples on the pond's surface. I'm happy to discover something beautiful in this new place—a heaven of sorts—in the middle of boredom and vast nothingness. A dock on the pond looks enticing, and I can envision myself dangling my feet in the water while soaking up the sun's rays. I decide right here and now that this will be my safe haven in a summer full of immense changes.

***

A few days have passed since finding my new hideout at the pond by the barn. I've read on the dock daily, having devoured nearly three books in four days during the afternoons and evenings before the sun disappears. I fear I'll exhaust my small personal library's inventory quickly if I keep it up.

I have also been brave enough—or bored enough, I'm not certain which—to dabble with painting again. Nicky happily let me into her stockpile of paints and new canvases. I set to work at the pond in the early morning hours just after my runs, painting it and its surroundings and trying to recall all the tips and tricks Nicky shared with me over the years. I have a long way to go but, so far, I've surprised myself with what I've accomplished on the piece. Nicky even commended my artistry, which meant a tremendous amount and gave a boost to my confidence level. I had given up painting when Eric came into the picture. It just didn't seem important anymore when I could spend my time with him instead, and the time away from it zapped some of my self-assurance.

I keep my phone by me at nearly all times, in the hopes that Eric will call at any moment. His scheduled calls have become unpredictable, with changes to his routine, and I can only assume that meeting friends, meandering around campus, and prepping for football practice are the culprits. It kills me to think he's enjoying college life already, while I'm stuck in this lonesome place.

I'd seen smug, body-bag-carrying Max plow up and down the road in his white truck a handful of times, but would leave for my runs only after I'd seen him go by, in hopes of avoiding him. This was intentional, in part because of my nervous reaction to him.

Truth be told, after a series of days stuck here in Nowheresville, I need an escape, a reminder that other people exist. Maybe I could even find a book or two in town. It is Thursday afternoon, and I figure Dad will need something from the hardware store for his to-do list. He'll be starting at the clinic soon, and I'm guessing he'll want to wrap up his projects.

Grabbing my wallet and keys from the desk of my small, old, may-as-well-not-decorate room, I head downstairs and out onto the porch. Dad is fiddling with the electric panel on the side of the house, his long fingers toying with the breakers.

"Dad?"

"Yup, Taylor?" He clears his brow of sweat and scratches his head.

"I was thinking of driving into town. Need anything?" He glances up at me, biting his bottom lip in thought.

"Actually, I do." He pauses to grab the yellow legal pad he'd carried out with him. Dusting it off, he writes:

1 can white outdoor primer
1 can white outdoor paint
1 4" paintbrush
1-lb 13-gauge 2-in stainless wood siding nails

"If you have trouble finding any of this, just ask someone who works at the hardware store to help you." He tears the list off the pad and hands it to me.

"Alright, I think I can manage that," I nod, folding the paper up and stuffing it in my pocket.

"I left my wallet on the coffee table. Why don't you grab some cash out of it?" he smiles at me, and I turn to walk off. "Taylor?"

"Yeah?" I turn back around.

"Thanks."

"Sure, Dad." I roll my eyes at him playfully and make way for the house, grabbing three twenty-dollar bills from his wallet.

Once situated in the car and having turned the ignition, I take a moment to place my long hair in a ponytail. I adjust it so that it's high on my head, and glance into the rearview mirror. *I need some color on my face.* I grab some rose-colored lip balm from the makeup bag in my purse and dab it on, then apply mascara to lengthen my thick lashes, followed by a pinch of my cheeks. *Much better*. I half giggle when images of a hazel-eyed Max and our odd introduction interrupt my thoughts. I have to admit he'd been funny, and fun wasn't something I'd encountered since coming to this farm on the outskirts of Schulenburg.

"Oh, Maxwell, Maxwell… how much longer will I avoid you?" Deep down, it would be for the best if I did continue to avoid him. No sense muddying the waters, with a boyfriend I love on the line, and college knocking at my door.

CHAPTER FOUR: CAUGHT OFF GUARD

Driving to town, I tried hard to recall the way to the main road. It seemed a never-ending maze of back roads. After having to turn around twice, I decide to trust my navigation system and finally find my way.

Schulenburg is much simpler than I'm accustomed to. I am more than surprised when random strangers extend a wave to me while I park in the spaces adjacent to the main street.

Strange—I don't know them. Small-town friendliness, I suppose.

Old buildings laced with ornate wood decorations line the street, something you don't see as much nowadays. Buildings' faded brick façades give away their age, evidence of their many years standing as time zoomed by around them.

I grab the hastily-scrawled list of items Dad needs just as the familiar Bob Marley ring jingles from my bag. I dig for the phone in my purse after setting the list on the console.

"Hey, you," I smile.

"Hi, love. How's your day?"

"Interacting with society again."

"No kidding; society, huh?" Eric chuckles.

"Yup, I'm sitting outside a hardware store. Got to grab some stuff for Dad."

"Well, country girl, I won't keep ya. Just wanted to say hi before I go work out." *Country girl, I hate the sound of it; city girl suits me just fine.*

"Love you, Eric. No country girl here, though. No way."

"Uh huh, you say that now, little lady," Eric laughs.

"Eric—"

He cuts me off before I can finish. "Relax, I'm kidding. I love you."

"I love you, too. Talk to you later?" I question.

"As soon as I can. Bye."

"Bye." I smile and end the call.

Oh, do I miss that guy. A kiss is so needed, but that won't happen. Coming back to reality, I place the phone back in my purse and smooth my snug, mint green, sleeveless button-up shirt. A hint of cleavage is peeking from it, but I don't care. I doubt anyone here will even take notice. I open the door and tug my short, dark denim shorts down a smidge after stepping out of the car. I reach back in to grab the list resting on the center console, and head for the store.

Opening the large, heavy door, I hear the jingle of bells and realize they are attached to it. The store's floors are wooden, and the place smells old, just like the farmhouse.

"Afternoon, hun," an elderly lady with large-rimmed glasses and bouffant hair smiles behind a tall counter.

"Hi," I nod.

"Can I help you, hun?" she asks as she pushes the glasses up on her nose.

"Uh, hardware?" I ask.

"Back left, hun."

"Oh, and books?" *I hope...pray.*

"Just a few behind you," she points out.

"Okay, thank you, ma'am."

"No problem." The old woman glances away at a stack of small papers—receipts, perhaps.

Glancing back at the tiny selection of books, consisting mainly of farmers' almanacs and gardening books, I decide not to waste my time, and instead tackle Dad's items first, heading for the back of the store. I wind my way through aisles of items I'm not accustomed to seeing all in one place, and locate a series of bins filled with nails. Bending down to decipher the choices at hand, I grab a box as a strangely familiar voice makes my stomach rise to my throat.

"Well, I'll be… Miss Runner." *Crap. Double Crap.* Breath leaves my body and I stand slowly, my knees shaky. I still haven't turned to look at him. "Shopping for nails? Must be bored," he chuckles as I force out a lungful of air and turn achingly slowly… unwillingly towards him.

A robust chest in a fitted, blue-plaid button-up shirt meets me at eye level. My eyes travel upwards to the handsome face I remember from a few days before, and dang it, he's even more gorgeous close up. Stubble covers his cheeks, and rich hazel eyes meet mine. *Speak, you idiot.*

"They're for my dad." I jingle the box and look down at the floor. This is not good. He's so handsome I don't even want to look at him. *Get yourself together, Sabian.*

"You were so feisty the other day… Taylor, right?"

Damn right I was, but now I feel like I've tucked tail and retreated to world's biggest wuss status. Eric's just as

41

handsome as this guy. Then it hits me like a ton of bricks—
boyfriend, Taylor, mention the boyfriend. I force my eyes
back up to his and my mouth feels like mush.

"Yes, it's Taylor." His mouth moves as if to speak, but
I abruptly intercede with what I'd failed to inform him
about upon our first meeting. "I have a boyfriend." His
mouth closes again into a straight line and he purses his
lips, as if trying not to laugh.

"Why does that matter?" he snickers. "I didn't know
talking to another human was a crime against
relationships." *Oh, why'd you have to go blurt that out,
Taylor?* It had seemed like a good idea, a defense
mechanism I suppose, like the spikes of a porcupine that
instantly engage at the sign of a predator. However, this is
one predator I'm not entirely sure I want to run away from.
Why?

"No, you're right." I soften my approach and meet his
eyes again. Flutters ensue, making me feel lightheaded and
off-kilter. "I'm sorry." I extend my free hand to him as I
catch him eyeing my chest. I clear my throat to gather his
attention, and his eyes leisurely rise back to mine.

"Last name is Sabian, Taylor Sabian." I feel a smile
plastered on my face, all the while wanting to slug him for

the full body look-over at the truck when we'd first met, and now the ogling of my cleavage. *Damn, why did I wear this shirt? Or is it really so terrible?*

"Like I said when we met the other day, name's Maxwell, but everyone calls me Max." He accepts my hand, enclosing it completely within his. His hand feels calloused and rough. "Pleased to meet such a beautiful girl, yet again," he continues.

I gasp, flustered, but he only surprises me further by kissing my knuckles gently with his soft but slightly chapped lips. Any desire I'd mustered to be friendly vanishes; he is too straightforward for my taste, and frankly, it makes me uncomfortable.

"Well, got to get the rest of the stuff I came here for." I tug my hand away from his and nod my head to one side, offering him a roll of my eyes.

"Oh… there she is—feisty Taylor. I like her."

"Well, *Maxwell*, if feisty keeps you in your place, feisty is what you'll get."

"Uh huh, well, I'm relentless, Taylor, and you'll get mad, out-of-your-mind bored here and need company—a friend. If you don't mind me askin'—if you'll still speak to me that is—where are you from originally?"

I force a deep breath to calm my nerves. "Houston, I'm from Houston. Matters because?" I start pacing the aisle, seeking the remaining items on the list in the hopes that he'll get the point. Instead, he follows like a lost puppy.

"Ah, doesn't matter; just curious if I can gauge how long you'll last before going mad in a town like this. See, I've seen plenty of girls from Houston at school and they wouldn't last two seconds here." He laughs, and I feel his smile like light beams through the back of my head, even though I'm not looking at him.

"And where is *school* exactly, Maxwell?" I feel cornered, with no means of escape.

"A&M."

My face falls and I turn back to him. As I stare him straight in the eyes, they cloud my brain. *What is the deal?*

"Texas A&M?" I manage, both pissed and elated. Not a combination of feelings I'm familiar with experiencing at the same time.

"What other Texas A&M is there?" Then I see the lightbulb in his brain light up as his eyes widen. "Ah, I've found you out. You go there, too?"

I squint at him and feel my cheeks tighten in irritation. "Not yet—starting in the fall." I turn back around and pretend to scour the aisles.

"So, you're what? Eighteen, then?" He again follows me.

"Yeah. You?" I can't help myself.

"Twenty-one."

Older, handsome, and won't leave me alone. Why did this have to happen now, in this time, in this summer?

"What are you lookin' for anyway? Maybe I can help."

Lovely, he wants to help, and all I want to do is run out the door because of the strange way he makes me feel. I relent. "Here." I shove the list at him.

"Let's see…" he taps his chin with the fingers of one hand while staring at the list held in the other. "Nails, check." He motions an imaginary check mark with his finger. "Paint brushes and paint. Follow me." He turns and his behind is just as appealing as his face. *Look up, Taylor.*

"Why are you here?" I question, and he stares back at me briefly.

"Welding stuff. Had to pick up some gear."

"Welding?"

Still walking, he proceeds to answer. "Yup, gate at my parents' needs some finishing touches."

He stops abruptly. I'm not expecting it, and fall into him, but he turns just in time, keeping me from an embarrassing stumble. He feels warm, firm, and smells like a combination of a woodsy musk and sweat. *Yummy.*

"Whoa, there." He helps to steady me, pushing me back upright, and then pauses an odd few seconds before releasing my waist.

"Sorry." I lock eyes with him.

"Here you go." He points to some cans of plain white paint and the brushes nearby. "If you need a certain color, they can mix it at the counter in the back of the store."

"No, white paint is fine." I break eye-contact.

"So…" he leans on the shelf near me as I pick up different paint cans to read their labels. "You free tomorrow?" He grins, knowing full well how much free time I must have.

"I… well… no." I avoid eye-contact as I pick up both cans of paint, holding one in each hand.

"Mmm..hmm…" he shakes his head, as if exasperated. "Here, let me get that." Grabbing the paint cans from me,

46

he saunters past, swinging them lazily. "Is that everything?"

I find the paintbrushes in somewhat of a daze, and he walks my items and me to the checkout.

As I rifle for the money in my pocket, he sets the paint cans on the counter and gives me a cocky salute. "I'll be seein' ya."

Before I respond, he swaggers off.

My heart is still pounding when I bring everything to the car, but as I scan the main drag for a bookstore, I begin to cool down and breathe normally again.

How long can I possibly avoid him?

CHAPTER FIVE: SUCKERED INTO A DATE

Strong hands trail my body, lavishing every curve. He grasps the nape of my neck and pulls me to him. His lips are so close I can taste his breath. Our lips nearly meet just as I wake. My heart thuds rapidly from anticipation. *It felt so real.* My thoughts shift instantly when the cell phone rings from the bedside table. I swipe my hair from my face before grabbing the phone. The clock on the bedside table reads six a.m. but it's Eric's ring.

"Hello."

"Hi, babe."

"It's early." My voice is scratchy.

"Yeah, I'm sorry, but we're starting training earlier now and I didn't know when I'd have another free moment."

I knew this might be the case going forward, fewer calls and less contact. I wonder what the fall will actually

be like when the season's in full swing and I'm dealing
with classes.

"It's okay. Thanks for calling."

"I'm trying, Taylor. I really miss you. You know that, I
hope."

"I miss you, too."

We talk a short while longer, but I find it difficult to
know exactly what to talk about; not something I'm used to
with Eric. We finally exchange our "I love you's" and end
the call. I want fresh air the moment I set the cell down,
and hurriedly pull on a yellow sports bra and running shorts
then lace my shoes and tiptoe down the stairs.

It's Saturday morning, and the house is dead quiet. It's
the last week of June and Dad has just completed his first
full week at the clinic.

I whisper to Judge on his dog bed, near the foot of the
stairs, "Come on, boy." He stretches his front legs, gives a
good shake, and follows me out the door. I decide to let
him run free of a leash; my loyal running companion.

I put my hair up into a quick bun and jet off, wasting
no time. We make the run down the dirt roads covered in a
layer of mist, and it's just cool enough to enjoy before the
heat of the summer day ensues. It's dream-like, the sun still

has not risen, and there is the occasional hoot of an owl in a tree. I have a surge of confusing emotions within me that I can't explain, and run until my legs ache. I see that Judge is tiring, so I decide to head home.

After getting back, the house is still lifeless. I fill Judge's water bowl to the brim, and he comes over to drink the freshly replenished water. I still feel flustered, but why? Is it that my conversation with Eric felt different? Judge lies down on the cool concrete of the porch after his drink as I ponder my thoughts.

Still trying to decipher my emotions, I make my way down to the dock and lay on it in a layer of salty sweat. The sun is just starting to crest the horizon, and I stare up at the sky as it does. I place my hands over my face and cry uncontrollably.

***

I awake on the dock, without any recollection of falling asleep. The sun is straight overhead in the sky now, blazing down over me. *What time is it? How long have I been asleep?* I sit up, dazed and with a splitting headache from the dehydration of both crying and running. The water of the pond makes me initially think of a quick dive in, but the layer of moss on its surface and the small fish swimming up-top quickly curtails my impulse as I stare over the edge of the dock. I'm a sweaty heartache of a mess, and opt to dip my hands into the water so I can cleanse my sticky face of sweat and tears.

After setting the house in my sights and walking back, I see a white, step-side truck at the house. Max's truck. *Here we go.* I look like crap, and really don't want to deal with his forward flirtatiousness right now. I hear laughter and conversation underway as I get closer. Dad is on the porch with Nicky, Pacey is climbing in and out of the bed of Max's truck, and Max is handing some sort of a dish to Nicky.

About to search for a hiding place until Max leaves, my presence is loudly announced by Pacey. "Taylor's back!" he yells annoyingly, pointing over to me. In unison, everyone on the front porch turns to me.

"Thank you *so* much, Pacey." I give him a searing look and cross my arms.

"Hi, sweetie. Were you at the pond? Thought you may have gone down there to read or something," Dad smiles. "We have a guest," he motions over at Max.

"Yes, I was at the pond, Dad. Max and I have actually met." I stop directly in front of Max and give him just as friendly a glance as I'd given Pacey.

"Oh." Nicky glances at me in surprise and offers a coy smile. I see Max give me another quick look-over of my body head to toe. I don't think anyone else notices.

"Yes, Mr. and Mrs. Sabian, we've met a few times now; once when she was runnin', and again at the store in town last week."

"Well, I'll be. You should've told us, Taylor. Max's mother was kind enough to send over a peach cobbler," Nicky smiles and holds up an ivory porcelain dish.

"Well, isn't that neighborly." I'm about to roll my eyes at Max, but he seeks me out first, slipping me a wink. I can't look away; his eyes have a hypnotic quality.

"Mom loves to bake, and asked me to drop it off on my way out of town, as a welcome of sorts," he grins, releasing me from his gaze and looking back to Nicky.

"Out of town?" I question. *Where is he going?*

"Yes, I head out every Saturday during the summer. Actually, that's part of the reason I'm here."

"Huh?" From the corner of my eye, I see Dad and Nicky smiling. They seem to be enjoying this too much, glancing in unison back and forth between Max and me.

"Yeah, my brother and his fiancée and I are goin' to a little dancehall outside of town this evenin'. Our uncle owns the place. Thought you might like to go, Taylor."

"Maxwell, remember, I told you, I have—" I was about to remind Max that I have a boyfriend, but Dad interjects.

"She'd love to, Max." I stare at Dad in disbelief then grit my teeth.

"Consider it done, then. I'll be back about five. We'll pick you up at six."

"But—"

Nicky interjects. "Oh, it's just what you need, Taylor," she assures me as I feel a slap on my back.

"What's Eric gonna think?" Pacey's hand leaves my back, and he spins in a quick circle around me.

"Pacey, shush." Nicky gives Pacey the evil mother eye. He stops immediately. Max looks generally unscathed by the mention of Eric's name, although I catch his jaw tense a brief moment.

What is the deal, people? Does nobody remember that I'm dating someone?

"Well, it was mighty fine to finally meet you folks. Glad there will be new life brought to this place. Your uncle was a great man, sir." Dad and Max must have already had the conversation about my uncle before I showed up. Max shakes hands with Dad.

"We're glad to be here," Dad says.

"Tell your mom thank you, Max. Can't wait to meet your family," Nicky smiles at Max and nods her head, the dish still in her hands.

"Yes, ma'am." Max tips the bill of his grey Texas A&M ball cap at her. *God, he's so good-looking with that tan skin and shimmering grin. Why?*

"See you this evenin', Taylor," Max beams, then cocks his head to the side and winks at me again.

"Alright," I sigh, pissed at all parties involved, but spellbound at the sight of him nonetheless.

Max walks back to his truck and drives off, just as I'm about to unleash the Spanish inquisition on my entire family. They are all smiling at me, and appear to be on the cusp of bursting out in laughter.

"What is it with you people?" I shake my head in utter disbelief while trails of dust appear down the dirt road as Max disappears.

"Oh, Taylor, honey," Nicky giggles. "You like him."

"I most certainly do not. In fact, I loathe him. And, Dad, what the heck was that all about? It feels like an arranged date or something."

"Taylor, honey, you need to get out of here. Be young. Have fun. Besides, other people are going, too, and we know where they live. They sound like nice folks."

"Yeah, great, now I get to explain to my boyfriend that I'm going out to a dancehall with a guy. Brilliant."

Dad cannot hide his smile and laughs. "Honey, you're young. Eric's off at school, and you can't stay cooped up here forever. Plus, you have something in common; you're both going to the same college."

"You people," is all I can manage. I walk hastily into the house and straight upstairs. The clock is showing 11:00. Holy smokes, I slept nearly three hours of my morning away down by the pond. I grab a fresh pair of clothes and head for a much-needed shower. Hidden from any family members in the bathroom, I laugh at myself in the mirror.

"Boy, this summer just gets stranger and stranger," I say to myself, but then my laughter turns to tears at how lost and confused I feel. How can my heart be so attached to a guy hundreds of miles away, yet want to jump the bones of a guy I barely know, out of mere physical attraction? It feels so wrong and so right all at once.

CHAPTER SIX: DANCE HALL

Well-rested, showered, and dressed in something pretty and sensuous, I feel more like a normal human being and less like an emotional basket case when six o'clock rolls around. My dark hair is blown dry and hangs in long waves over my shoulders. I have on my brown cowgirl boots with a denim skirt, and a fitted red and white checkered shirt tied in a knot at the waist. I haven't been able to dress up in what feels like forever now. I find it refreshing, and I'm curious what Max will think.

I toyed with whether to text Eric or leave him a voicemail, but couldn't bring myself to do either. I'd deal with it later. I still wasn't sure how to bring it up. Surely he's not doing anything much different from this? He's mentioned going out with groups of people. It just feels funny, though, and I can't place why I feel bad about it. I'm still pissed that everyone around me has encouraged the current predicament I'm in. I know Dad would never steer me wrong, yet I have to listen to my conscience, too.

It's just a friendly night out, Taylor. Stop beating yourself up.

Sitting on my bed and looking in the small makeup compact mirror, I brush a little blush on my cheeks followed by a dab of lip gloss. Just as I finish, I hear the roar of the now-familiar white pickup truck and raise my eyes to look through the beveled glass of my bedroom window to see Max drive up.

I take a deep breath and tell myself aloud, "Have fun, Sabian; you deserve some fun. Don't feel bad; it's just friendly."

Continuing to look out the window, I see Max and who I assume is his brother exit the truck with an attractive redheaded young woman. Max and his brother look a lot alike. Both have tanned skin and light brown hair, but Max has a few inches on his brother. The only other obvious difference from a distance is that Max hasn't shaved, his rugged stubble still evident, while his brother is clean-shaven. *I love that stubble.*

Both of the guys are wearing perfectly pressed jeans, polished boots, and pearl snap shirts. I find the attire unexpectedly attractive. I'd grown so used to Eric in a football jersey or a polo shirt and shorts. They were two completely different styles, but I could definitely get used to this cowboy look.

The redheaded woman is beautiful, even from a distance, in a flowing pink blouse, snug white jeans, and brown embroidered western boots. She stands tucked against Max's brother's side, her arm around his waist. I set my eyes back to Max and see Judge run up to him. He bends over to scratch the lab's ears. Pacey is not far behind, and Max gives him a high five.

"Taylor!" Nicky hollers from downstairs. "Max is here."

I close my eyes a fleeting moment. *Alright, here we go.*

I gather my purse and proceed downstairs. Nicky and Dad are on the porch, shaking hands with Max's brother, when I exit the house through the creaking front door.

"Wow, you look great," Max gushes, with a killer smile. I unwillingly smile back. His eyes linger on my exposed waist.

"Well, thanks." I'm flattered.

"Well, little brother, you've hardly done her justice." Max's brother grins, displaying perfectly pristine teeth.

"Taylor, this is my brother, Collin, and his fiancée, Emily."

"Hi, Collin." I reach out to greet him with a handshake and he reciprocates. His shake is firm but friendly. His fiancée follows, shaking my hand with a welcoming smile.

"So nice to meet you, Taylor." Emily nods her head with a close-lipped smile. Her ring glimmers as we shake hands. *Wow! What a rock!* I've only just met her, but she gives off a genuine vibe, relaxing me a little.

Max turns to Dad as Collin, Emily, and I complete our greeting. "I'll have her home by midnight, sir."

"Oh, no worries; stay out as long as you'd like." I stare at Dad, flabbergasted. I feel my mouth hanging open, and see Nicky slip me a wink. *This is new. I've always had a curfew.*

"Well, thank you, but we'll still make sure she's back at a decent hour, Mr. Sabian."

"You kids just have a good time." Dad shakes Max's hand, and the four of us make for the truck. Max beats me to the passenger door and opens it. I climb up into the passenger seat. Collin opens the door for Emily as well, offering her a hand as she climbs into the backseat then settles in next to her, shutting the door. *Sweet.* Max walks back to the driver side, hops in, and fires her up. I wave to Dad and Nicky as we pull away, and there is Pacey, same as ever, throwing that damn ball up and into his catcher's mitt.

The truck smells like a mixture of hay and cologne, but it's very clean, immaculate even, with a tan leather interior and a nice radio displayed in the console. The stereo is playing some country song at a barely-audible volume. I find it surprising that Max can keep the truck so pristine living out here.

Collin is no holds barred, and starts in with the questioning right away. "So, Taylor, I hear you're headed to A&M."

"Yes, Collin, I am," I laugh and shift to face him and Emily. I catch Max glimpsing at me in the process. Knowing his eyes are on me makes me flush.

"And you have a boyfriend?"

Uncomfortable.

"Geez, Collin." Emily slaps his shoulder with her perfectly manicured hand. "Could you be more blunt?"

"Yes, I do. His name is Eric." I shift in the front seat.

"Where is he?" Collin questions further. Emily glares her eyes at him.

"He's in Kansas, K-State; got a football scholarship. His whole family went there."

"Huh, ain't that something? What position does he play?"

"Tight-end," I say without hesitation, football having been engrained in me, especially being the girlfriend of a star player.

"Collin, give the girl a break," Emily comes to my aid. "Ignore him, Taylor." She grins.

"It's alright." I smile back at both Collin and Emily. Turning back, Max's eyes meet mine. I feel the now-familiar flutter in my belly.

"Well okay, party poopers." Collin squeezes Emily's shoulder gently and laughs. He strikes me as the humorous one in Max's family, probably the jokester.

"I have some questions," I interject.

"Shoot, Sprout," Max winks then tickles my exposed navel swiftly with his strong fingers. Something deep within me comes to life with desire.

"Sprout?" I punch Max in the shoulder.

"Yup, teensy little thing; good name for you."

"Okay, whatever. Now, my questions. What's your major, Maxwell?"

"Veterinary medicine."

Wow, I wouldn't have guessed that.

"Ha-ha, she called you Maxwell," Collin laughs contagiously. Emily giggles, too.

"Yeah, I know; she can't seem to help herself." Max shakes his head at his brother in the backseat through the rearview mirror.

"What do you do, Emily?" I question, turning to face her.

"I work in marketing for an online fashion company." She pulls her long fiery locks over one shoulder. Collin slips her a soft kiss on her exposed neck. They seem very much in love.

"That sounds like fun." I smile.

"I enjoy it. I've been with them since I graduated from Baylor two years ago."

"Where did ya'll meet?" I ask.

"We met at school," Collin picks up the conversation.

"So, then, what do you do, Collin?"

"The family business."

"Which is?"

"Oil and gas."

"Oh; explains the big house." I realize I've just said that aloud. "I'm so sorry, that was rude."

"No, it's not. It's the truth," Collin retorts.

"You're not going into the family biz, Maxwell?" I ask.

"Nope; I've wanted to be a vet ever since I was a kid."

"I think it's great to know what you really want to do." I envy him. I have no clue what the heck I want to do. I wish something piqued my interest, but I have no idea where to start. Right now, I plan on going to school only because it's what I feel I'm supposed to do. An undeclared major will have to suffice for now.

"My parents were…disappointed that I didn't venture into the business, like my other two brothers, but they respect my decision and support me."

I glance up at Max and we exchange yet another brief smile. The four of us engage in conversation the remainder of the car ride to the dancehall. I learn that Collin and Emily live in Dallas. They are both twenty-three, and they will marry in the fall at some posh affair in the heart of Dallas. Their oldest brother, Aiden, lives in Houston. He's twenty-eight, and he and his wife are expecting their first child. All three brothers graduated from Schulenburg High

School, but went to different colleges. I find myself strangely respecting all of the boys, knowing they'd come from a small town, but were all doing so much with their lives. It made me question all of the presumptions I'd had about a small town. After all, I come from Houston and have no idea what I want to do with my life.

***

We pull up in a dusty parking lot.

"This is a dancehall?"

"Yeah, why?" Max laughs. It was slightly smaller than I'd expected, and the parking lot was fairly empty.

"I guess I just thought it would be bigger."

"Well, fancy pants, it's not Dallas or Houston, you know."

"I'm sorry, you're right." I realize I sound rude, and see Max recoil a bit, something I haven't seen him do before.

"Ha. I said that the first time Collin brought me here, too. It's pretty low-key. Typical neon lights, beer, and country music." Emily says, making me feel less awkward about my comment.

"Our uncle owns it," Collin adds. "Half is a bar with a small dance floor, and the other side is open for large dances. Tonight there is no big dance."

"Oh. Okay." I look back at Collin and then next to me at Max.

We all pile out of the truck and head for the door. Max clasps my hand as we step inside the low-lit, smoke-filled room. I feel a small jolt of electricity jut up my arm at the touch of his warm hand. Collin and Emily are right behind us. Max guides me to an empty table with four chairs. We all sit down.

"Drinks, people?" Collin asks.

"Coke," I say without hesitation.

"Coke?" Collin laughs. "How 'bout a beer?"

"But I'm not twenty-one." I can't drink yet, not legally.

"You don't have to drink, Taylor. Collin can be persistent," Emily comes to my defense.

"Yeah, don't push it Collin," Max glares at his brother.

"First—why, yes, Emily, I can, as you know, be persistent. I got you, didn't I? And second—our uncle owns the bar, so it's a little different," Collin winks at Emily then glares back at Max, followed by a smile at me.

"Get the girl a Coke, Collin. I'll have a gin and tonic," Emily instructs.

"I'll just have a Shiner Bock," Max requests.

"Alright, alright," Collin puts his hands up in surrender and leaves for the bar surrounded by an accolade of neon lights.

"Thanks for coming. I hope you have fun," Max says to me from across the table.

"So far, so good," I smile back at him.

"Just a second," Max gets up and walks over to an old jukebox. *Man, I haven't seen one of those since I was a kid.* Emily and I are left alone at the table.

"You know, Mr. Max over there is pretty smitten with you." Her breath smells like minty chewing gum, and her glossed lips sparkle under the dim light. She places her hand lightly on my forearm.

"Excuse me?" I cock my head to the side, wondering if I heard her right.

"I can read it all over him," she grins. *Oh, Lord, it's worse than I thought.*

Max reappears before we can continue, and I hear *Neon Moon* playing from the jukebox. "Shall we?" He reaches for my hand, and I reach for his. He guides me to the low-lit dance floor. We are the only people on it. He wraps his hand around my waist and takes my other hand in his. My free hand graces his shoulder. Though he's much taller, everything fits perfectly as we're dancing. He leads and I follow, and it oddly feels like we've danced together a million times before. We step in unison, and he twists and twirls me every few steps. It's freeing in a way, and I'm thoroughly enjoying it. I wasn't expecting that.

"Where'd you learn to dance? You're pretty good."

"Or you're just a good leader," I laugh. Truth was, I had always enjoyed dancing, and it seemed to come naturally to me, but Eric didn't have it at the top of his list of enjoyable pastimes. I hadn't realized until that moment how *much* I enjoyed it.

Pressed so closely to Max, I smell his cologne and inhale slowly, taking him in for once instead of putting up my defenses. I haven't felt anything like this before, and I can't put my finger on what exactly feels so different. The song comes to an end, and Max twirls me one more time, winding me to him. I chuckle, and he does as he'd done at the general store and kisses my knuckles.

"Thank you, Taylor." He smiles down at me and then places his hand on the small of my back as we walk back to the table. By the time we return, his brother has drinks waiting. I'm thankful, as I'm a little thirsty from the dance. I take a long, hard swallow and feel my throat burn.

"What is this?" I cough.

"Coke," Collin laughs, "with Crown."

"Collin, what the hell?" Max gives him the evil eye.

"I'll get you something else, Taylor," Max moves to take the drink, and I'm instantly reminded that it was my own dad who'd said to have a good time. I'd been through a lot these past weeks, and it wasn't like I'd never had a drink before. My mind was made up.

"No; it's fine, Max. But thanks." I take the drink back from Max's hand.

"Are you sure?"

"Yup, I'll be fine."

***

Two hours, two Crown and Cokes and a beer later, I'm feeling some kind of good. I've danced with Max at least five times. I can't contain my giggles. Max is leaned back in his chair, enjoying my conversation with Collin as I feel my words becoming more slurred.

"So, tell me about when you knew Emily was *the one*?" Collin's arm is draped over her shoulder, their chairs pulled closely together.

"Did you really just ask me a mushy question? That's girl stuff, you know."

"Oh, no; let's hear it, hot stuff." Emily laughs. Alcohol appears to have left her slightly buzzed but still coherent.

"'Fess up, Collin."

Emily and I grin, ready to burst with laughter. He looks at me and smiles. "To be honest, I just never wanted to be with anyone else. See, our parents always told the three of us boys that it's not the person you can live with, it's the person you can't live without." I wasn't expecting his answer to be so deep, yet I can see the truth in it.

"Well, that's awfully sweet, Mr. Collin. I'm impressed," I offer.

Emily looks at him with sincerity and they exchange a soft kiss on the lips.

I hear the door open behind us, and a group of people clamors in to find a table. There are two girls, perhaps slightly older than me; one a cute blonde, well-dressed with a sparkly belt, the other with dark hair in a curled ponytail. There's a rather good-looking guy with them. I take notice that Max is trying his best to look anywhere but in their direction. I eye back and forth between him and the table, and then Collin nudges my shoulder and waves his finger for me to lean in close.

"What?" I whisper, mixed with an uncontainable alcohol-fueled giggle.

"See the blonde over there?"

"Yeah." My curiosity is piqued.

"That's Max's ex from high school. He broke the poor girl's heart. Now she goes to the University of North Texas. But I don't think she ever got over our Max here."

"Ohhhh, uh, oh." We wrap up our conversation just as the blonde approaches our table, and rests her hand on Max's shoulder. This inwardly makes me cringe. I don't expect this reaction.

"Hey, Max. How are you?" she leans in to give him a side hug.

"Hi, Brittany." He looks anything but comfortable, and I'm trying to contain my smile at his noticeable anxiety. I bite my lip. The forward Max I'm accustomed to has vanished.

"Who is your friend?" Her blue eyes sparkle behind a few layers of mascara, the total opposite of me.

Collin interjects sarcastically, "Hi, Brittany." She waves and, in what seems to be annoyance, replies,

"Oh. Hi, Collin."

"So good to see you, too, Brittany," he laughs and motions as if toasting his beer to her. Emily ignores her. I sense she doesn't like Brittany.

"This is my friend, Taylor," Max turns and says straight into her face, but he looks irritated.

"Nice to meet you, Taylor." She nods, but avoids eye contact with me.

"You, too, Brittany." I look directly at her, emboldened. *I'll play this game.*

"Maybe we can dance later?" she questions Max, never having looked at me. *Awkward.*

"We'll see," Max replies plainly.

"Well, nice to meet you, Taylor. Good to see you, Max." She offers one last smile and Max's face holds a straight line.

"Bye, Brittany," Collin waves, fighting a smile. Emily shakes her head at Brittany, obviously annoyed.

"Bye," Max adds, but doesn't look at her as she walks back to her party's table.

"Why is she here? It's not even a busy night. Must be home visiting her folks or something." He looks uncomfortable.

"Hey, just chill out. If Sprout over here gets tired, I'll dance with you, Max," Collin grins, and I can't control my laughter.

"Oh, yeah, sure. Thanks, Collin," Max stares at Collin and takes a swig of beer.

"That's what big brothers are for." He pats Max on the back, and now I'm nearly rolling, with my head between my knees.

"That girl's a hot mess. Parting ways with her was the best thing you ever did, Max," Emily affirms.

After a few minutes pass and the laughter subsides, Collin goes for another round of drinks. Without reason, other than being brave from alcohol, I hold my hand to Max's cheek and brush his stubble with my thumb. He leans into my hand, and I suddenly realize it wasn't a wise idea. I continue anyway.

"Hey, we'll keep her away, okay? Let's go dance." He smiles and then offers his hand to me.

"Alright, let's do it." We head back for the dance floor. *When it Rains* is playing.

***

We've danced another hour, and I'm now three sheets to the wind. I've been spun, twirled, two-stepped, and waltzed, and am having a good ol' time. We've also managed to keep Miss Blonde Shiny Belt at bay. I do, however, realize that the alcohol is gaining on me and, after a dance, I lean into Max's chest, feeling a bit dizzy. He leans down and whispers in my ear, "Let's get you home. Your dad is gonna kill me, bringin' you home like this." I pat his chest.

"Maxwell, I'm…fine," I slur.

"Oh, no, you're not, but you don't know it yet. Let's go, Sprout." I lean against him and we walk back to the table.

Collin goes to wrap up the tab, I think, and I remember to grab my purse from the chair. I hear Emily argue with Collin. I don't catch much, except to hear her mention that he never should have bought me so many drinks. I'm pretty sure I walked out the door, because the smoky smell and sound of music have stopped. I have to lean against Max to stay balanced. He's warm, and I desire to be near him more than I ever have since we've met. He lifts me into the front seat and closes the door, and I press my forehead against the cool glass of the window, now finally feeling the effects of my night of fun.

Any attempt to close my eyes leads to dizziness, so I force them back open, even though I'm tired. After what feels like double the amount of time getting home, we pull up the dirt road to the house and Max parks. Everything feels half real and half dream-like, but it's all starting to spin faster now.

"Need help getting her inside?" I make out Collin asking.

"I'm so sorry, Taylor," Emily sounds concerned.

"No, I think I'll be okay." Max climbs out of the truck and opens my door. I slump into his arms. "Taylor, you okay?"

"I don't feel so good." My stomach is churning and I know what's coming.

"Hold on." He sets me down and lets me lean against him. I feel him pull my hair back as I throw up all over the ground. Two rounds later, Max asks, "You feel a little better now?"

"Oh, my parents are going to kill me," is all I can think to say.

"No, Taylor, your parents are gonna kill *me*, but I'm gonna kill my brother first." He picks me up, and I lean my head against his chest. He feels warm and comforting. He walks me to the house, and I hear him quietly manage to open the front door somehow. I don't make out any signs of life. *Whew*. "Where is your room?" he asks quietly.

"Upstairs, on the left," I manage. He walks with me in his arms up the steps, sets me gently on the bed and then disappears. He returns a short time later with a glass of water.

"Here, take a few sips of this." He brings the glass to my lips. "I'd say I hope you had a good time, but I guess we'll see what you think when you wake up tomorrow," he chuckles softly.

I take a few swigs of water; it tastes bitter in my mouth but I swallow it anyway. I lay my head back on the pillow and he takes the glass from my hand. I don't remember anything else after that.

CHAPTER SEVEN: HANGOVER

"Ugh." My head is throbbing and I have a foul taste in my mouth. I grab the sides of my head with both hands and curl my knees to my stomach. *Am I wearing the same thing I was last night?* I lean over the side of the bed and see my boots perfectly placed together on the floor and, sure enough, I'm still in my denim skirt and checkered top, with my belly still exposed. The sun is shining through my window. I squint from the bright light. I sit up slowly, anticipating that my stomach may not cooperate. I lean up and see a trash can next to the bed, too. *Who did that? Max?*

I start to remember him carrying me up the stairs, and wonder if Mom and Dad know. Boy, are they not going to be happy. Maybe this is one way to nix the Max issue. But is he an issue? I like him. Sort of. Right?

"Why is this so confusing?" I question myself aloud.

My stomach growls. *I'm hungry.* After the grumble subsides, I sit up fully and see a note on the desk near my window that I didn't leave there. I reach for it from the bed and open it.

By the time you read this, you may not feel the greatest, but know that I had a great time and hope you'll come out again sometime. Had a blast!
Max

I'm thinking this is both sweet and irritating. How is it possible to loathe and like someone all at once?

Ugh, I need a shower. I place the note by my pillow and grab my phone from my purse. Surely the charge is low. I'm stunned to see four missed texts from Eric. *Oh, no.*

The last text received reads:
Where are you? Are you ok?

I've got some explaining to do, but I don't even want to think about it right now. First, I have to face Dad and Nicky. I grab a fresh pair of denim shorts, a cream fitted tee, and a bra and underwear and go to head downstairs. I open my bedroom door and hear people talking in the kitchen, but I think I hear Max. *What the hell? Am I dreaming?*

I very quietly walk down the steps, trying to figure out how to bypass the kitchen, but knowing I have to go by it to get to the bathroom. I finish the steps and bolt past the kitchen entrance, but am stopped by a voice.

"Taylor?" It's Dad.

"Uh huh." I wince. Ever so slowly, as if being dragged, I walk backwards to the kitchen entrance.

"Yes?" I peer around the corner, only to see Dad and Max drinking coffee at the kitchen table.

"Heard you had a good time."

"Uh—yeah?" I cringe as I see Max, with his killer smile and a fresh set of clothes. I can only imagine what I must look like. Walk of shame for sure.

"Hi, Taylor." Max tips his coffee cup up to me.

"Hi; why are you here?" I am still only exposing myself from the neck up in the doorway, intending to hide evidence of my bra and underwear in hand.

"Just wanted to make sure you were okay." Max eyes me intently.

"Uh, how am I supposed to respond to that?" I glance back and forth between Max and Dad.

"Oh, Max told me," Dad laughs.

"What?" I'm thoroughly confused.

"That you had some drinks last night."

"And you're not royally ready to read me the riot act right now?"

"Taylor, honey, do you really think your mom and I don't know what's coming when you get to college?"

"Uh, aren't you supposed to be red-faced mad right now, Dad?"

"Well, I could be, but Max was kind enough to come by this morning and let us know. He even brought you some breakfast tacos from town." I see Max smile at me and he slips me one of his damn winks.

"What is wrong with you people?" I shake my head. "I'm going to take a shower." I can't deal with their crazy, unexpected reactions right now.

I walk steadfast for the bathroom door, shut it with a slam, and turn on the shower faucet as hot as I can get it.

***

Half an hour later, I emerge from the bathroom, still with a queasy stomach but feeling fresher. I hope Max has left, but there he sits, bright-eyed and bushy-tailed with Dad—and now Nicky—at the kitchen table. The only spot open at the small table is next to Max. After heading straight for the sink and filling a glass with water from the tap, I sit at the table.

"Here you go." Max pushes a taco wrapped in tinfoil over to me. I am starving.

"Thanks," I sigh as I feel all eyes on me. "Any salsa?"

"Sure." Max unveils a few small single-serving cups from a paper bag. *Of course he came prepared with salsa. What else would I now expect from Mister Ten Steps Ahead of the Game?*

"Did you have fun last night?" Nicky asks coyly, wearing a white button-up shirt, jeans, and perfectly placed hair; as usual. I glance over at Max, who's grinning from ear to ear. I try, but I can't lie.

"Yes." I don't want to elaborate.

"Well, that's good," Dad answers. He's smiling at me over his cup of coffee. I eat the taco slowly as Dad, Nicky, and Max talk like they've known each other for years. I suspect Pacey must still be in peaceful slumber in his room, as there has been no sign of him. The whole situation is just weird, and I feel like I'm totally missing a piece to this unexpected puzzle, with them chatting so normally. As I finish my last bite of taco, I go to the garbage can and dump the foil in the trash. I turn back to everyone.

"Thank you, Max." I nod and head for the front door.

"Where you headed?" Max sounds surprised.

"For a walk."

"Can I come?"

"Okay," I don't know what else to say, so I immediately surrender to his request. He follows me outside; Judge is sunning on the lawn. I whistle, and he immediately responds.

"Where to, Sprout?"

"The pond," I reply as Judge takes his place at my side.

"That's a really good dog." He smiles down at me with his handsome grin.

"Yup, he's a good boy." I pat Judge's head and hear the jingle of his tags.

"Are you okay? I mean it." Max's eyes penetrate mine as I look back up at him.

"Yeah. I feel a little gross; my stomach, I mean. But the breakfast taco really did help. Thanks."

"Yeah, no prob. Talk to Eric?" he asks in an uncomfortable tone.

Whoa, wasn't expecting that.

"No, he's texted like four times. I haven't responded."

"You didn't do anything wrong, Taylor. College won't be much different; outside of school, I mean. And you're a babe, so he's gotta know guys will swarm you."

"Is that supposed to be a compliment? You're pretty blunt, you know."

"I just see what's before me, is all. You're hot." He raises an eyebrow and gives me a cocky half-grin.

"Whatever." I nudge him with my elbow.

"Can I ask a question?" he asks then presses his lips together momentarily.

"Well, since you've told me I'm a babe and hot in the last two minutes, how can I not comply?" I laugh.

"Why on earth do ya'll have so many pieces of art in that house?"

"Couldn't miss it, huh?" I giggle. Due to a current lack of storage space, Nicky had placed artwork on every possible wall space. "Well, my mom, Nicky—she paints. They're building a big room for her to paint and store them in in the new house they'll start in the fall, but she just doesn't have the space for all of 'em right now.

"Well, that explains it, then." Max tucks his thumbs in his jean pockets.

"So, you like the pond?" Max questions.

"Yeah; it's my only getaway here. I'm sort of painting it right now, too."

"Wait. What? You paint, too?"

"Uh—a little. I quit a few years back. But now that I have soooo much time on my hands, I figured, why not?"

"I think that's pretty neat. Show it to me sometime?"

"Maybe." I don't want to relent completely. I don't want him to think he's winning me over.

"I used to fish at that pond with my brothers when I was a kid. Your uncle used to let us come over whenever we wanted to drop a line in."

"Oh. I didn't know that. Actually, I didn't know him very well at all."

"He was a good man." I'm slightly warm inside from his sincerity.

"So, would you go again? Dancin', I mean." I ponder a second before responding. We've now halfway reached the pond.

"You know, I think I would." I stare up at him. "I really had a good time." He surprises me by reaching for my hand and giving it a quick squeeze. I give a quick squeeze in return then release his hand, afraid to convey more with the touch. We walk the rest of the way in silence and go sit on the dock as Judge goes to sniff the banks.

"So, you said you head out of town every weekend. Where do you go?" This is something I've been dying to know. He laughs and gives me a gargantuan smile.

"I think I'll keep that a secret for now."

"Why is it a secret?"

"I just think it might come in… handy one day."

"What is that supposed to mean?" I'm lost.

"I don't know. Something just tells me to keep that one quiet for now.

"So, you're really a serial killer," I joke.

"Maybe." He forces a serious face, and then busts out his always-alluring smile. I slug his firm shoulder.

I unlace my shoes, take off my socks, and dangle my feet in the water.

"You know there are snakes in there, right?" Max gives me a creepy eye.

"What?" I pull my polished toes out immediately as he begins laughing uncontrollably.

"That's not funny, Maxwell."

"Really? I thought so. It's true, but I'll make you feel better about it. They won't bother you." He takes off his boots, stuffs his socks inside them, and rolls up his jeans. He dips his feet in, and I slowly slip mine back in, too, though more carefully inspecting the water this time.

We spend the next several hours talking like old friends. I just don't get how I can feel like someone I've just met has been a part of my life all along.

CHAPTER EIGHT: RAINY DAY

"So, I was at a dancehall in town. I didn't hear my phone ring, and crashed when we got back."

"Sounds like fun; you need to get out." Eric is acting so coolly to this. "Who did you go with?" I can't fib, even a little. We've always been so honest with each other.

"Well, I met a neighbor. His name's Maxwell." The phone line goes eerily silent.

"Eric?" I feel nervous jitters in my stomach.

"It's fine, Taylor. You don't have to explain everything to me. We have to trust each other to make this work." I exhale a heavy breath into the phone.

"It's not like that, Eric; not at all. I love you, and I miss you. He's just the only other person around for miles, and it's sort of a relief to be around someone close to my age."

"How old is he?" Eric asks.

"Twenty-one." Another moment of strange silence and then his response,

"Okay, look, it doesn't matter. I love you, and you've trusted this relationship enough for me to go hundreds of miles away and still try to make it work." I'm quickly reminded of the night he left in the rain, and feel my heart sink at how much I hated saying goodbye to him in the flesh. I miss his warmth, his security.

"So, you're okay, then, with me hanging out with Maxwell?"

"Do I really have a choice?" I'm suddenly irritated, and know that I just need to get off the phone before this takes a darker turn.

"Look, I'll wait for you to call. I know your schedule is crazy now. I miss you. Sweet dreams." I hear him breathe heavily into the phone.

"Alright. Have a good night." He hangs up without so much as a goodbye or our always-said "I love you".

Why should he feel upset? I'm the one stuck out here, he's the one who left for school a zillion miles away. I don't have a friend in sight right now, except Max. What's worse, I really do actually enjoy spending time with Max. Damn, why does this have to feel so strange from every angle?

It's been a weird day; waking up with a hangover, my parents being okay with it, enjoying an afternoon talking with Max, and wrapping it all up with a mad boyfriend. I just need some sleep. I surrender to my bed, wrap myself in a blanket and pull it over my eyes, wondering what to make of it all.

***

Two weeks have passed and it's now the early part of July. The days have been abnormally soggy and rainy for a Texas summer. Confined to the house more than I care to be, I finished the painting of the pond. I'm proud of my efforts. It has sparked my inspiration to paint more—a fire that I believed had fizzled out. My creative desire is reignited. The Fourth of July was spent curled up on the couch as rain poured down outside. Max had asked if I wanted to go to a neighboring town for a Fourth of July dance despite the rain, but I lied and said that I didn't feel well. I was afraid to muddy the waters further with Eric, especially since there's obviously a physical pull to Max that I can't ignore; one that he reciprocates. I didn't talk about Max again with Eric, and it seemed as if our conversations went back to normal, except for the fact that they seemed to lack depth.

I still feel our love; it's just that our connection seems different, changed. I don't know how to regain ground, with our lives so far apart. For now, I just choose to let love guide me and trust that our relationship is strong enough to push through this.

Maxwell unexpectedly shows up at the house Saturday morning, and from my window, I see him pull up the drive. This strikes me as odd, since he always goes somewhere on Saturdays, though I still don't know where. Curiosity is killing me. *What could it be?* Despite my efforts to avoid him, Maxwell resurfaced the previous week after our talk at the dock. He came over to help Dad mend some fence line and roof shingles. Even more puzzling, Dad appears to really like him. I'd said hello when I saw him, but I had hesitated to derail from small talk. He just makes me feel so damn bewildered inside and I don't know how to interpret it.

As rain hammers down, I meet him on the porch in my matching grey cotton camisole and teensy short pajama set. My hair lies against the small of my back. He's already soaked just from the jog from the truck. His hair is wet at the tips, and his skin glistens. It's enticing and only adds to his handsome features.

"What is it?" I glance up at him, barefoot and chilled from the cool rainy air. I apply friction to my cold arms, clammy from the rainy mist.

"I wanted to see if you'd like to go up to A&M tomorrow. Rain's supposed to stop. I need to drop off some furniture my parents wanna get rid of at a house just off campus that I share with some guys."

Inside, I'm jumping up and down at the prospect of escaping the farm. I'd also get to see my future alma mater. All the while, however, my gut sends beacon-like signals to my brain to avoid Max for Eric's sake. *Go for it!* my inner, brave Taylor screams.

"Sure." I can feel my smile stretching so wide it hurts, and bite my lip in an effort to erase it quickly.

Max laughs and places his hands softly on my arms. He takes over the task of warming my arms, gently applying friction over my goosebumps. His gesture makes me feel desired, churning sensations deep within me.

"Alright, then." He grins down at me. "Go get dressed." He stops rubbing my arms, applies a single, tender squeeze to my biceps, and releases me.

"What? Why? I thought you said we were going tomorrow?" I feel my eyebrows furrow.

91

"I wanna take you over to my house." He quirks one eyebrow and offers a devious smile.

"Huh?" I'm really dying to go, but fight like crazy against my better judgment. I lower my head.

"Oh, come on, Taylor. Nothing funny, I promise." He raises my chin lightly with his finger. "I just want you to meet my parents, and thought we could watch some movies. It's a rainy day. Not much else to do."

I close my eyes. *This isn't that difficult. Just say yes, Taylor.*

"Okay. Give me a few minutes. Why don't you come in?" He gently strokes the bottom of my chin and then releases me, igniting a thousand shivers down my body. He steps inside behind me. "Have a seat." I motion towards the leather sofa in the living room. "I'll be right back."

I run upstairs, pull on a long-sleeved navy blue V-neck tee that offers enough cleavage to gather attention without being too obvious, and pair it with fitted—very fitted— jeans, then slide on a pair of flip flops. I decide to leave my purse and cell phone at home.

I'll just be up the road anyway, and how awkward would it be if Eric called while I was at Max's?

I run downstairs to Nicky and Dad's room. They're both getting ready in the small bathroom. "I'm headed to Max's house. Be back later today."

"Okay, Taylor." Dad glances over with a shaving-cream-covered face, and Nicky smiles around a mouthful of toothpaste. I head straight for the door.

"Okay, ready when you are." His eyes are fixated on the painting sitting on an easel next to the sofa. It's the one of the pond that I'd just completed. I'm still uncertain of what to do with it.

"Is this the pond painting you talked about?" he points to it.

"Yeah; I just finished it."

"It's good—amazin', actually." He looks surprised. "You have talent."

"Uh, not sure about that. I'm not that good compared to most—especially not against Nicky's work. Now, *she's* talented."

"Well, Sprout, I think you have a gift." He looks over to me. His gaze penetrates mine. I bite my lip to hide my smile.

"Let's go." He stands and grabs my hand unexpectedly, and we exit the front door, running to the passenger side of his truck. He opens the door and helps me climb up. I feel my wet feet slip on the edge of the floorboard, but his hand helps me balance as I maneuver inside. After he shuts the door and runs back around to the driver's side, now half-soaked, he starts her up and slowly drives down the dirt road drive.

We approach an old crossing not too far down the road, with a shallow stream of water flowing over it. I've gone over it several times running and never thought a thing of it. Max slows the truck.

"Is this normal? The water going over the road."

"Yeah, when it rains. It's fine in my truck—for now—but see that gauge over there?" He points to a white wood post alongside the crossing, with markings every foot.

"Yes."

"When it's at one foot, don't cross it… ever. It will pull you right over the road and into the creek."

"Well, that's certainly good to know. All these little things we city folk never have to think about."

I emphasize city folk and receive a narrowing of the eyes, followed by a smile. He drives on once we've passed the crossing. Not more than two minutes later, we pass through a big wrought-iron gate boasting a large B in its center. Past the windshield wipers, I see the house beyond the tree-lined drive. It's much larger than it appears from the road, and reminds me of something in an old movie, with southern plantations on the set. Massive white pillars stand out, even through the soaking rain pouring down.

Max pulls right up to the front door in the circular driveway. "Got as close as I could." He glances at me from the driver's seat.

"It's fine. Really." We both climb out of the truck and run to the tall front door.

He reaches for the knob and opens it. We slip inside and he closes the door gently. Immediately, I remove my shoes, my toes now painted crimson red, and then take a long look at my surroundings. The house is enormous, with polished wood floors that stretch the entirety of the downstairs I can make out, and vaulted windows letting in the rainy, grey hue of the day. It's like something out of a magazine. I soak it in, relishing its beauty and comfort; something I'd had a piece of in my old home in Houston, and something I'd fail to enjoy in the new home due to being at college. I feel a tug at my hand.

"Taylor?" I look up at Max and realize my mouth is hanging open in wonder.

"It's amazing." He smiles and laughs at my reaction. I nudge his side. He grins, and I can't help but smile back at him.

"Maxwell?" I hear his name called from the other side of the house.

"Maxwell? I thought you hated that."

"Hell, yes, but it's my mom. She has this thing with callin' me by my full name; ever since I was a kid."

Now I don't feel that bad. I love the ring of 'Maxwell', and still enjoy the fact that it perturbs him when I use it.

"Uh huh." I wink at him as a dark-haired woman, dressed impeccably in white linen pants, a magenta button-up top, and perfectly applied makeup, surfaces down the long hallway from the back of the house. Her hair is placed neatly in a low bun and slightly teased on top. I know where Max gets his beautiful smile now, but his dad must have the lighter colored hair, because hers is much darker than Max's.

"You must be Taylor." Her eyes are an intense, but stunning, green. She reaches to hug me when she gets close.

"Hi, Mrs. Bara." I reciprocate her gesture and hug her back. She stands back and clasps both of my hands in hers.

"You are such a beautiful young lady." She jiggles my hands in hers. To make me comfortable I think.

"Oh, thank you." I smile graciously at her as she releases my hands.

"Well, welcome, and please make yourself at home. Wish the rain would stop so you kids could go swimming."

"You have a pool?" I look up at Max.

"Yup," he says, looking back at me.

"Well, nonetheless, I have a roast on in the kitchen, so ya'll have some later today. Okay?"

"That sounds amazing; I'd love to," I gladly accept.

"Where's Dad?" Max asks his mother.

"He had to make a last-minute trip to Houston for business. Left right after you did."

"Bummer; I wanted him to meet Taylor."

"Well, hopefully next time, honey." She smiles at Max with a mother's love.

"Alright, well, I'll give Taylor the grand tour."

"Okay, and again, make yourself at home; everyone is a friend here." She smiles once more at me, and then Max pulls me away by the hand as she turns back in the direction she'd appeared.

***

After what seems like eons of looking around the house, I'm in envious awe. They have over five bedrooms, four bathrooms, and every other room you can fathom—from his mother's crafting room to a media room. Max completes the tour by showing me his bedroom.

"So, this is it. The humble abode." I follow him into his room. His walls are painted a rich hunter green, I see Schulenburg high school memorabilia on a bulletin board, and A&M posters are spread out on the same wall. His bedding is navy blue and covered in a stack of clean laundry.

"Laundry?" I giggle at him.

"Yeah, one of the perks of bein' home for the summer. Won't get that treatment next summer."

"What do you mean?"

"Hopefully, I'll be accepted into the veterinary school at A&M. I probably won't come home in the summers after that."

"Oh." I'm unexpectedly saddened by the thought of him not being here next summer, especially if I *had* to come back. I change the topic. "So, what movie did you have in mind?"

"Well, let's go see. We have a ton down in the media room."

"Alright." I follow him back downstairs to the media room, admiring the view of him. His ass sure looks amazing in jeans. After entering a darkly-painted room, he opens a closet full of DVDs. "Wow, you weren't kidding."

"Ha, no," he laughs. "You pick."

"Okay." I scan the limitless movie selection and decide. "Hmm, what about... this one?" I pull one out and hand it to him.

"Dumb and Dumber?" He jiggles it above his head.

"Yup." I offer a half-smile. He walks over to an enormous television that encompasses half the wall and puts the DVD into the player housed nearby. There are two large sofas in the room, and we both plop into the first one, as it sits in front of the other. It swallows me up. He props his feet up nearby.

"Hey, now, don't play couch hog," I giggle.

"Oh, please, like you need that much room, Sprout."

"Oh, shut up." I throw one of the pillows behind my head at him. He simply grabs it, puts it under his own head and replies,

"Well, thank you."

"Just start the movie." I roll my eyes at him.

"Alright, alright." He turns the television on and starts the movie. We end up watching movies all day as the rain pours down and pounds against the roof. Three movies later, I feel my eyes get heavy and give in to the urge to fall asleep.

***

I feel large arms around me. My eyelids flutter open and the bright blue screen on the television reminds me where I am. The heavy arms draped about me are Max's, and my back is to his front. How did we end up like this? I can't recall how this happened, but don't want to move. He feels firm and warm and, for the first time, I desire more from him. It makes me elated, yet sick inside at the same time. I feel his heavy breath on the back of my neck and know that he is still deep in sleep. I trace the outline of one of his large hands draped over me. They are soft on top and rough on his palms. His breath on the back of my neck tickles and sends goosebumps from my neck down my arms. I release his hand, sit up slowly, and lay his arm gently back onto the couch.

Able to stare freely for once, I take in the sight of him. His face is so defined and handsome, yet ruggedness from his stubbly cheeks gives him a hardy quality. How can I look at him as such an exquisitely handsome creature and still love my Eric? I am beyond confused. I carefully slide to the other end of the couch, unwilling to give away what I'd woken up to as Max stirs from sleep and yawns deeply.

"Hey, beautiful. How long have I been out?" *Ah, hell, here comes flirtatious drive-me-out-of-my-mind Max.*

"I don't know, Maxwell. I just woke up, too."

"Boy, you're a gorgeous sight," he pushes further.

"Would you stop it, already? You know I don't know how to react to that."

"You need to learn to take a compliment, especially when you're about to embark into a sea of guys at school who will think just the same as I do. You're beautiful, Taylor, and that Eric—let's just say he'd better have hung the moon."

I plot to do as I'd done earlier and reach for another pillow behind my head, but Max is ahead of me this time, taking me by total surprise and swooping in. He picks me up then sets me on the floor, tickling me until I want to cry.

"Okay, okay, mercy....mercy!"

I'm grabbing for his hands but they are moving too quickly to catch, so I grab his arms instead. They are firm and chiseled beneath my grasp.

"Say it."

"What?" I giggle

"Say, 'I'm beautiful'."

"No...no."

"Say it, or I'll tickle you to death."

"Okay...." I can barely get the breath out. "I'm beautiful."

He stops abruptly.

"There, was that so hard?"

He stills over me and our eyes lock. Everything gets eerily quiet. I feel an energy drawing me to him, but Eric flashes through my mind and I roll over and push myself to my knees. *What to change the subject to?*

"Didn't your mom say she wanted us to go down later for her roast?"

He shakes his head and gives a sideways smile, appearing annoyed. "Uh, yeah. She did."

He stands up and reaches down, offering his hand to lift me from my knees. I accept, and we make our way down a long hallway, heading downstairs for the kitchen.

The light through the windows has faded to darkness, but I cannot tell if it is still raining. I follow Max down the stairs, and the amazing aroma of the roast is mouthwatering.

"Oh, wow. That smells so good."

"She can make a mean roast, my mom." Mrs. Bara is sitting on the couch in the living room nearby the kitchen, flipping through the channels. A large grandfather clock in the corner of the living room is showing six-twenty. *Wow, we literally spent all day upstairs.*

"You kids hungry?"

"Oh, my goodness, yes, Mrs. Bara. This smells divine."

Max walks over to his mom and gives her a quick squeeze on the shoulders. "Thanks, Mom."

She looks at him with the full breadth of a mother's love, and I can tell in this moment that his parents raised him right.

"I set the bowls out by the crock pot, so dig in," she smiles over at me.

***

It's late when Max drives me home. I have a full stomach from Mrs. Bara's scrumptious roast and feel the energy regained from our nap wearing off. The rain is now a sprinkle, and the gush of the water has subsided over the crossing we'd passed earlier. Near the gate, Max suddenly slams on the brakes. The truck hydroplanes in response and we jolt back and forth before coming to a halt. I'm panting at what has just unfolded.

"Are you okay?" Max looks at me in the dark light of the truck. He's placed his arm across my chest. His hand grazes my breast. Desire flares, and my heart pounds at the unexpected stop and his hand on my chest. I can decipher the whites of his eyes. He slowly—too slowly—lowers his hand.

"What happened? What is it?"

Before he responds, I see the culprits running outside. They are barely visible, but with just enough features to make them out—dogs.

"What the…?"

"They're probably wild dogs." Max looks out the back window.

The pack is now fading into the wet darkness down the road. He turns back to me and stares sternly, straight into my eyes.

"I know this is the last thing you probably wanna hear. More rules, especially after already hearing 'bout the flooding. But you need to be careful when you run. They're out here more than you may think." Max places his hand on my shoulder, as if to make sure I'm paying attention.

"Okay." Good grief, this place is a death trap. "Is there anything else I need to know about while we're at it?" I inquire, bothered at the thought of crazy dogs attacking me, and irritated that nothing here seems simple.

Max pulls his hand to the wheel. He slowly lifts his foot off of the brake and steps on the gas.

"Nope. Think we've covered the bases for now." He gives a quick nod and drives to the house. The porch light is on. I reach for the truck door handle as Max comes to a stop.

"Can I ask you something?" Max asks before I manage to open it. I look over my shoulder at him.

"What?"

"Do you think you ended up here this summer for a reason?" His tone is sincere, his hazel eyes genuine. I'm unprepared, and look away from him to the droplets on the windshield. *Where did this come from?*

"I don't know, Maxwell. If I'm going to be honest, I was really unhappy to be coming out here. It's just that so much has happened since graduation. Going to college is one thing, and I'm happy to go. It's just that I had to leave everything I knew all at once. My mind knew this was coming, but my heart wasn't ready." I am still staring out the windshield, into the dark, very aware that this could get uncomfortable, and my attraction to him doesn't help.

"So, that's how you felt when you got here. What about now?" I still see Max's face pointed towards me from the corner of my eye.

"It's not so bad." I grin with ease and turn back to him. Our eyes meet. "Now, can I ask you something?" I question.

"Okay?" He moves his right arm from the steering wheel and rests it on the seat behind my head.

"Where do you go?"

"What do you mean?" The mischievous smile I've seen when asking him this before emerges.

"On weekends, where do you go?" I say firmly, knowing he knows full well what I'm talking about. He plays games or ignores the subject whenever the question arises.

"Ah. I'm still keepin' that a secret." He tugs his lower lip with his teeth then releases it as he drums the fingers of his right hand on the seat.

106

"Why? Something you don't want to tell me?" My curiosity is burning.

"Nope. Nothin' like that. Maybe one day I'll show you." His hand lightly brushes the skin of my back as he pulls it back to the steering wheel. It makes me shiver.

"Now, you'd better get inside so you can get a good night's rest. I'll pick you up at nine tomorrow morning, if that works for you."

"I'll figure out your little secret, Maxwell," I giggle and turn for the door.

"Don't you have a boyfriend to call?" Max replies to my challenge with an annoyed undertone. *What an asshole thing to bring up.* My heart suddenly leaps in my chest. *Eric, dammit.* I haven't had my phone with me all day. He's probably called or texted. Then I process that Max is either trying to piss me off or change the subject.

"I guess so," I say shakily.

Unprepared, I realize that I truly enjoyed every moment I had with Max today, and it makes me feel a tinge of guilt. Breathing deeply in through my nose and out through my mouth, I finally open the door and slide out to the soggy grass.

"Want me to walk you up?" Max starts to open his door but his jaw is tightened, something I now notice that he does when perturbed.

"No, I'm a big girl." I slam the door shut and rush to the front porch. My flip flops slide over the wet grass, so I slow down to avoid slipping as drizzle dampens my hair.

"See you in the mornin'!" I hear Max yell from the truck, in a still irritated tone. He must have lowered the window when I ran to the house. With my stomach turning in knots at the feelings rushing through my mind—and, surprisingly, my heart—I don't respond. I go straight to the door without glancing back.

I hear the truck pull away and walk to the dark kitchen, flipping on the light and filling up a glass with water at the old porcelain sink. My mouth is dry and I take a sip. I look out the window directly above the sink and see Max's truck lights growing fainter down the road. My heart thumps like a bass drum in my chest as I rehash the day.

I feel funny every time I'm around him. He makes me frustrated, giddy, and wanton all at once. It's great to know I have a friend here, but I feel things when I'm around him that I've never felt for Eric, as if I could kiss him and not think twice. How can this be, when I gave my innocence away to Eric the night he left for school? I didn't think twice about that either. Now I doubt myself entirely.

The sound of Judge's nails on linoleum breaks into my thoughts as he enters the kitchen. He walks over and sits at my side, resting his head against my thigh. I set the glass down and scratch his velvety-soft ears. He looks up at me as I ask aloud, "What's wrong with me, Judge?"

CHAPTER NINE: FEELINGS

"Are you sure you want to do this, Taylor?" Eric looks down at me with his grey-blue eyes. I run my fingers through his thick, dark hair. He's resting above me, propped up with his elbows in the back seat of the truck.

"Very," I say, without hesitation. He leans down, his lips meeting mine. It's late, and rain pours down heavily outside. We softly, sweetly, make love for the first time, the only time, before he leaves for Kansas State.

***

I sit straight up in bed, breathing heavily. My hair trickles over my shoulders, covered by a white, oversized t-shirt. It's dark outside. I feel for the phone on my bedside table—2:15. Did I really just dream that? It was so real, just like the night it happened.

With blurred eyes from the bright light of the phone screen I text Eric. It's late, but I don't care.

Are you up?

I type and hit send. No response. I glance at the screen for minutes. I give up at two-thirty a.m. and set the phone back down. I roll over and wrap my body around the pillow between my arms and legs.

Our conversation before bed had been interesting. He's probably mad. I had told Eric about spending the day with Max at his family's house, and had explained that it was rainy, with nothing else to do. I told him that we just watched movies. Eric didn't get verbally upset, per se, he just didn't say much. I've learned over the course of our relationship that a quiet Eric often equals an upset Eric.

About to doze back to sleep, *Could This Be Love* rings from the phone. I smile and reach for it, answering as I raise it to my ear.

"You okay?" Eric's voice is rough. Oh, if he were here right now. The desire for him from my dream is still fresh.

"Yes," I sigh. "I just had a dream—about the night you left." I bite my lip, curious what he'll say.

"That was some kind of great, wasn't it?" His voice is a whisper, but still raspy.

"Yes, it was. I just wish you were here so it could happen again." I giggle and move to my back, facing the ceiling.

111

The moon is shining through the window and casts shadows above me. As bright as the moonlight is glowing, the rain must have ceased.

"I would reply in kind, but I have a roommate, you know."

Duh, Taylor. I completely forgot.

"Oh, you're right, I'm sorry. I just needed to hear your voice." I press my eyes closed and reopen them. "I'll let you go. Thanks for calling."

"I love you," he yawns into the phone.

"I love you, too, Eric. Bye." We both hang up.

I reach and set the phone back on the bedside table, now wide awake and craving a glass of milk. Sneaking quietly downstairs, I see a small lamp lit in the living room. Who could be up at this hour?

A creak of the stairs gives me away.

"Taylor?" Dad's voice asks softly. Rounding the landing, I see Dad on the couch with some notes in hand.

"Hey, Dad. Why are you up?" I adjust my pajama shorts that have twisted to one side, and run my fingers through my hair.

"Notes from the clinic." He holds them up briefly. "Couldn't sleep, so I figured, what the hay? You couldn't sleep, either?"

"No. I just want a glass of milk." I nod in the direction of the kitchen.

"Are you doing alright, Taylor?" Dad asks sincerely, and sets the notes down on the coffee table.

"Yeah, why?" I'm lying, and he knows me too well to not know it.

"You know what I mean, hun. Are you and Eric okay?"

I shrug my shoulders.

"Here, come sit down." He pats the couch seat. I relent and curl up on the opposite side of the soft leather sofa.

"I'm trying to figure all of this out, Dad." I locate a blanket nearby and pull it over me, a little embarrassed I'm in only the shirt and short-shorts, though the tee covers me to my knees. "I feel kind of funny talking about this with you, if I'm being honest," I smile nervously.

"I get it, Taylor. It's just that I'm your dad, and it's my job to care about you. That will never stop. After your mom passed away, you were all I had. I know this move happened quickly, and I know Eric went far away even

113

before that. It was a lot, and I appreciate you rolling with it. I know it's been tough on you."

"Yeah, the move stunk. But worse, I wish Eric's family wasn't as tied to Kansas State as they are. He's so good he could've played football here, too." I feel tears building in my eyes, and breathe deeply to press them back.

I don't want a crying session with my father. Dad lays his hand on top of the blanket where my foot is and gives it a quick squeeze.

"Sometimes things happen for a reason. I know that when you're eighteen you believe you have it all planned out. Maybe whatever that plan is will work out, but don't be afraid of what will happen if it doesn't. Maybe something greater lies ahead."

I meet his eyes, still fighting back tears. I didn't expect this conversation at this time of night.

"I don't know if I have a plan, and I realize I'm only eighteen and it's a big world out there. I just didn't expect to move all the way out here—"

"And meet Max," Dad finishes before I can. I nod yes.

"He's a nice young man, Taylor."

"I know you like him, Dad." I cock my head to the side and offer an annoyed look.

114

"It doesn't really matter what I think. It's not *my* heart. Both Eric and Max are nice guys. Don't dwell on it too much. You'll figure it all out."

"Thanks, Dad." I slide over and give him a hug. He kisses the top of my head before I rise from the couch and head back for my intended mission: milk from the kitchen. Dad resumes reading his clinic notes.

CHAPTER TEN: HAPPY ESCAPE

I sleep in as late as I can, tired from the dream, phone call, and conversation with Dad in the middle of the night. Nicky and Dad are all for the trip up to College Station with Max, though I didn't mention it to them until just before he was supposed to arrive.

The amount of freedom they allow where Max is concerned makes me curious. Curfews are non-existent since moving out here, although the likelihood of getting into trouble seems minimal, minus the alcohol incident. What I do know is that they sure don't seem worried about me spending time with Max. I'm just so apprehensive about what he makes me feel.

While getting ready, I make up my mind to relinquish avoiding him after all that has occurred in the last twenty-four hours. I've recollected my first time with Eric while spending an entire day with Max. If I were confused before, it's only worse now. Max and I will be at the same school in the fall, and our families live so close.

I'm relying on Dad's advice to trust that I will figure it all out. I just pray I can do it without hurting anyone in the process. I don't want to hurt anyone. One thing I have decided is what to do with my recently-finished painting.

I am waiting on the porch when Max arrives at nine a.m. sharp, with a large brown couch strapped in the bed of his truck. Judge is lying down by my feet. The sun shines intensely, and the humidity is suffocating from the previous night's rain.

"See you later, boy." I acknowledge Judge, with the painting in hand, and step off the porch. My white Keds squish on the ground. I've taken the time to style my hair this morning and have added slightly more lip gloss and mascara than usual. My tight powder-pink top and favorite denim shorts are already sticking to my freshly-showered skin. As I head for the truck, Max climbs out.

"Mornin', pretty thing," he smiles, dressed in faded jeans and a fitted blue t-shirt. It's the first time I haven't seen him dressed in a button-down shirt, and the fitted t-shirt makes his chiseled arms stand out. His stubble makes him look years older. I like it.

"Morning, yourself." I stop in front of him and glance up. "This is for you." I offer the painting to him. I'm unsure of myself after our departure last night, and it feels like a way to break the ice of any residual tension.

"Are you serious?" he smiles, admiring the painting and taking it from my hands.

"I can't really think of another place for it and, since you took such a liking to it, I figured it'd have the best home with you." His eyes leave the picture and find mine. Our eyes don't part for several seconds.

"Well, I have my purse; should I bring anything else?" I say, peeling my gaze away from his. It's not easy. I could stare at him all day.

"Nope, we'll be back later today; should be fine. Your parents know we're goin', right?" he cocks his eyebrow.

"Yep. Ready when you are."

We pile into the truck and Max places the painting delicately in the back seat before we head out. After we reach the highway, Max breaks the awkward silence that's ensued since we left the house. I think he's unsure of my mood from the night before, and I'm not sure of myself around him. Max reaches for the radio playing alternative country, and turns it down.

"Listen, I'm sorry if I upset you last night. No one gets me wound up the way you do." He glances over at me then returns his eyes to the road.

"No, I'm sorry. I just wasn't sure how to respond. You make me nervous and anxious all at once." I glance out the window at the other cars on the road, afraid to look him in the eye. I'm startled when I feel his hand cover mine. It's warm. I glance down at his hand just as he pulls it back to the steering wheel.

"I don't ever want you to feel uncomfortable around me, Taylor. I understand you don't wanna do anything that'll hurt your relationship, and I don't wanna screw up our new friendship."

Finally, he's said something to define our situation. It's refreshing.

"I appreciate that. I didn't mean to make you feel bad. I'm just trying to figure out how to make everything fit together so it all makes sense."

"Believe me, Taylor, you fell outta the clear blue sky. I come home for the summer, plan on welding a little here and there for money and helping my parents out around their place… I didn't expect to be doin' this right now; startin' a new relationship, no matter the context."

"Ditto." I finally look at him and he looks back. My heart melts at the way he smiles at me. *Why does this happen?* I force my eyes back out the passenger window and change the topic.

"That girl the other night at the bar, how long did you date her?"

"Brittany?" Max laughs.

"Are there more than just Brittany?" I question, raising my brow.

"No, not really; we dated about a year at the end of high school. I've dated girls at A&M, but nothin' serious." He runs a hand through his blond-streaked hair.

"Did you love her?" I don't hesitate to ask. *Holy hell, why did I ask that?* Max doesn't respond right away. I look at him, embarrassed. He taps his fingers a few times on the steering wheel then purses his lips. "You don't have to answer that. I wasn't thinking. I'm sorry." I shake my head.

"No, it's okay. And no, I didn't love her." He looks at me plainly then back to the road and continues, "I thought I did, but I didn't understand the gravity of it then. She met someone else right after we each left for college. I was upset but not heartbroken. I realized then that I didn't love her. She called me a few months later and wanted to get back together. I told her I didn't want to, but wished her the best."

I ponder his response and wonder if this will be Eric and me. I'm torn. My heart is diverting in a million directions and I don't know which direction is right.

"I see," is all I can say.

"Look, things don't always work out the way we think, Taylor." Oh, Lord, isn't this what dad had just said in our middle of the night pep talk? How weird.

"Funny, I just heard that recently," I huff.

"From Eric?" Oh, I'm sure Max wishes this.

"No; my dad, actually." I rest my elbow on the door and adjust my head so I'm looking at Max.

"Your dad, he seems like a real great guy. Your mom, too. And that Pacey, he just cracks me up. I had his energy as a kid." He smiles as he mentions them.

"Yeah, Dad and Nicky are great. Pacey, on the other hand—well, he's my little brother. I can be annoyed if I want to. I love him, though."

"Nicky? Why do you call her Nicky?" His crinkled eyebrows display his confusion. I realize I haven't ever explained our relationship to him.

"I call her 'Nicky' and 'Mom'. She's not my biological mother," I sigh and continue, "My real mom died when I was two. I don't remember her, but Dad says we're a lot alike. Nicky married my dad when I was four, and she's always treated me like her own."

Max glances back and forth between the road and me a few times.

"Well, that explains a little bit."

"What's that?" I smirk.

"Why you don't look like her at all. You're so teeny and she's so tall. Your dark hair and eyes versus her blonde hair and light eyes. You have your dad's colorin', but that's all I gathered between the two of them."

"They're good parents. I'm lucky. Eric's parents, on the other hand, well, let's just say they are unhappily married and will never get divorced." I remove my elbow from the door where it had been resting, and sweep my styled hair behind my shoulders.

"Yikes, that's sucks," Max responds.

"Tell me about it. His family is like a legacy at Kansas State. The men have all played football there, going back to his grandpa. His parents met there, too. I guess they were happy, but things went south at some point. Eric didn't go home very much near the end of high school, and we spent a lot of time together when he wasn't on a football field. A full scholarship and escaping his bickering parents were reason enough for him to leave, I suppose. He could've played football somewhere in Texas, I'm sure, but he didn't."

"How do you feel about that?" Max asks.

"Sad. But I guess absence makes the heart grow fonder. Isn't that the old saying?" I twist a long section of my hair in my fingers and look out the windshield at the white clouds in the sky.

"I'm not trying to start a fire, but he was a fool to go so far away from you. If you ask me, you're worth stickin' around for."

My heart nearly stops. No one's ever said anything like that to me. I turn to Max and lightly place my left hand on his right shoulder,

"Thank you, Maxwell. That's really sweet." I rub his strong arm with my thumb a few times then release it. Every inch of me wants him to pull the truck over so I can kiss him—hard. *What is wrong with me?*

***

We pull into College Station just shy of eleven. I see Kyle Field on the A&M campus before anything else. It's enormous against everything in the quaint college town. Students must be in town for summer classes, and walk around carrying backpacks. A few others are jogging or talking in groups. *I can't wait for this.*

"How far do you live from campus?" I ask.

"Just a few blocks. We'll be there in a sec." He smiles over at me. "This is the happiest I've seen you since we met."

"I'm definitely ready for this," I grin wide-eyed.

"You'll love it here," Max chuckles.

We leave the roads near the campus and venture down a few side streets. Max slows to the curb in front of a small white house. There are lawn chairs in the yard and a big A&M flag and Texas state flag are hanging from the front porch.

"My roommates are here for the summer, so you'll get to meet them. Plus, they're gonna help me get this big boy into the house," Max points back at the couch with his thumb.

"Alright." This is what I needed; a day's escape from the farm, a trip to my upcoming alma mater, and time to figure out the looming question of what I feel about Max.

***

A half-hour later, I've met Max's roommates, Sam and Grayson. They're both going to be seniors. Sam is a business major, and Grayson studies oil and gas engineering. I can tell they are fun and witty—both have a hell of a sense of humor.

Max and Grayson have just finished moving the couch into the living room with an array of other un-matching furniture. I posted up at a stool by the bar, glancing at posters of Texas bands and a dartboard, waiting for them to finish.

"Here, I'll show you my room," Max walks over and takes my hand to help me off the stool; except he doesn't let go. I follow him down a small hallway to the room at the end. He opens the door.

"Madam," he grins, and offers for me to go in ahead of him. The room is very simple and surprisingly clean. A large bed is centered with a small desk and dresser strategically placed in the room, I assume to utilize space.

125

"Very nice," I wink at him. "You must have a great decorator," I laugh.

"Oh, yes. The very best of course: me." He grins and looks down at me just as my cell phone rings from my purse. I'd picked it up when we left the living room. It's Eric's ring.

"Sorry. Excuse me a second." I look at Max. His face is unreadable. I locate the phone in my purse and head for the front door of the house, hoping for a little privacy. I answer the phone just before reaching the door.

"Hello," I say, walking onto the small porch.

"Hi, beautiful," Eric sounds giddy.

"Hey. What's up?"

"I was just thinking about your call last night," he laughs.

"Kind of random, I know. I'm sorry, but I was thinking about you and couldn't help myself," I respond as cars pass on the street. One of them honks the horn.

"Where are you?" Eric asks.

"I'm in College Station today."

"Really? Good for you," Eric says encouragingly. "Just decided to head up?"

"Uh, sort of." *Here we go. Things are going to get awkward again.* "My neighbor, Max, had to drop something off at his place here. He offered to take me with him."

"Oh," Eric's enthusiasm leaves his voice entirely. "Well, have fun. I'll talk to you later."

"Wait—" The phone goes dead before I can say anything else. *Damn.* I hear the front door open behind me.

"Everything okay?" Max asks. I muster up a happy face.

"Yeah. It's okay," I say, turning towards him.

"Are you sure?" Max questions. "It was Eric, wasn't it?" I nod my head yes.

"Hey, you're not doin' anything wrong, Taylor." He lifts my chin gently to meet his eyes.

"I know, but why do I feel so bad?" I get lost in his eyes for a second. He removes his finger from my chin.

"You're about to embark into a brand new world very soon. He's gonna have to get used to you being around other people. Shit, this was partially his choice, remember? Besides, he's already at school. Doesn't he go out, too?" Max inquires. His neck has reddened.

"Yeah. He mentions it every once in a while. He's started practice now, so that takes up a chunk of time, too."

I hate feeling like a bad person. But am I really doing anything wrong?

"Hey, let's go grab a bite to eat. What do you say?" Max changes the subject and I'm glad.

"That sounds good." I force a smile.

"Oh, wait," Max moves from the porch and out to his truck.

"Where are you going?" I grin, following his handsome body with longing eyes.

"I have a picture to hang up in my room before we leave," he smiles back at me after reaching the truck and removes the painting from the back seat.

***

We are now almost home from College Station, having left for home a few hours before. The sky is changing colors with the setting sun. Although it's been hours since lunch, I'm still stuffed to the gills. Max had introduced me to the Dixie Chicken across from campus for a burger and, boy, was it good. Afterwards, he offered to walk me across campus and we searched out the dorm I'll be in. We talked for hours about everything, comparing our youth; one in a big city, the other in a small town. What I realized is that, despite our different upbringings, we share a connection I can't yet define but that's undeniably growing each day between us. Not to mention he can make me laugh till I want to cry sometimes. Being with him feels effortless. Yet, I'm also struggling to clear the conversation with Eric from my mind the entire ride back. Everything feels so awkward with him, and I hate it. It's never been like either of us to be angry with the other or feel so much friction. Max has been nothing but kind to me in a summer that would have otherwise been painfully boring.

I force the array of feelings I'm processing aside when I see the white farmhouse, and Max slows the truck and turns into the gate. I let out a sigh without meaning to.

"Penny for your thoughts," Max says.

"Just thinking about today. Thank you—so much."

"Anytime," he answers and stops the truck in front of the house, putting it into park. Judge is waiting on the front porch, exactly where he was when I left that morning. I see Nicky and Dad through the kitchen window, eating dinner I assume. I'm anything but hungry right now.

"I know we just got back, but would you like to go for a walk?" I ask. "I'm still full and not ready to go inside."

"Sure." Max turns the truck off and we both exit. Max puts his keys in his pocket and I go to set my purse on a chair on the front porch. Judge rises. His tags jingle as he follows me back to Max waiting in the yard.

"Where to?"

"The pond." It's been so wet and rainy I haven't had a chance to go to my place of solace. We make the walk together, and Judge stays with us. I dodge mud puddles and stick to the grassy edge. "I failed to consider how muddy it would be. I'm sorry." I look over at Max.

"Don't sweat it; these aren't my nice boots."

"Yeah, but I've got my white shoes on." Not bright on my part. I concentrate on carefully placing my feet. We're close, but the mud is getting worse.

"Here." Max sweeps me up in his arms in one swift move.

"Wait. What are you doing?" I ask.

"Now you won't have to walk in the mud," he smiles down at me.

"But I'll get heavy." I wrap my arms around his neck to help support my weight.

"Yeah, right, all ten pounds of you, Sprout. We're not far anyway." His arms are strong and make me feel safe.

Judge is splashing through puddles as Max carries me. We pass the barn and arrive at the pond. Max gently sets me down when we near the foot of the dock. It feels like a long way down.

"Thank you. We could've just turned back," I say to him.

"I know."

"So, why'd you do it?" I question.

"Because you wanted to go. It makes you happy here. And cuz it's gonna start raining again tomorrow."

"What? What is with all this frickin' rain? It never rains this much in Texas during the summer." I'm disappointed. I am *so* over the rain.

"Farmer's Almanac says a wet summer this year. What can I say? Mother Nature has other plans," Max laughs.

"Why exactly do you read the Farmer's Almanac?" I cross my arms across my chest.

"Oh, you know, for the hell of it," he jokes. "Actually, my parents keep it around to know when to plant their fields and my mom's garden."

"Okay, I guess I'll accept that answer." I nudge his shoulder.

Judge is chasing a grasshopper and is thoroughly enthralled. I walk to the edge of the dock, and Max follows. We sit at the end as we've done before, but the water is murky from the recent rain. We don't take our shoes off this time, just sit facing each other and talk until the sun is about to disappear.

"We need to get back so we're not walkin' in the dark," Max says.

"Let's boogie," I say as Max reaches his hand down and helps me up. We walk back to the bank.

"This time, let's piggyback it, little lady," Max turns backwards.

"Good Lord, I'm going to have to get a running start," I laugh.

"I'll squat," Max offers.

"Okay," I giggle. He lowers a bit and I jump up onto his back. "You'll be ready to enter a marathon with this workout," I can't help but add.

"I don't do the runnin' thing," Max replies matter-of-factly.

"Such a shame," I snicker.

Halfway back to the house, his breath gets ragged.

"This is ridiculous, Max. I'll walk. I can wash my shoes. You're getting tired."

"Here, I'll set you down a sec." He bends his knees and lets me slide down gently to the muddy ground. Judge sniffs everything around us when we stop.

"You gonna make it, old man?" I look up at him.

"I'll manage just fine, young lady," he retorts and tucks a piece of my hair behind my ear. The sun is almost completely gone; just a low purple light remains.

"I'll walk; don't worry, Maxwell." I start walking before he can pick me back up again, but can barely make out the road.

"Look, I can carry you. Really. Stop bein' so damn stubborn."

"I swear, Max, you can be such a pain in the a—". My foot sinks ankle-deep into wet mud. "Uh, oh."

"What?"

"I stepped in mud….and I can't get my foot out." I wiggle my foot beneath me. It doesn't give. "Ew." I don't like the feeling of wet mud oozing into my now-ruined shoe.

"Hold on." Max walks over to me. "Here, take my hands. On the count of three, I'll pull." He stands in front of me and I place my hands in his. Max holds them firmly, counts to three, and pulls. When he does, my foot doesn't budge. Max pulls harder, and I feel myself catapulted towards him. He loses his balance and we tumble backward to the ground and into the mud. My shoe stays in the muddy hole.

"Oops," is all I can manage. I feel mud splattered all over me. It's almost dark now, and I can make out only a few of Max's features. I've landed on top of him. "I'm so sorry, Maxwell."

"Well, I guess next time I *should* carry ya, because now you're down a shoe and I'll have to carry ya anyway. Now who's the pain in the ass?" Max quips.

I can't help myself, and begin to laugh uncontrollably. Max does the same. When the laughter subsides, we lock eyes. I haven't moved and feel the length of his body underneath me. I brush his cheek with my thumb without thinking. Max props himself up on his elbows. We are now nose to nose. I feel an electric current roll through my body head to toe. My heart is pounding as I feel his warm breath on my face. Desire ignites with sudden fury. I know what comes next. I can't let it happen.

"We should go. We'll hardly be able to see now." I take my thumb off of his cheek and hear the jingle of Judge's tags nearby. I roll over and slowly stand up, one foot shoeless. Max gets up after me. "I'm so sorry you got mud on you," I apologize.

"I think I'll live." Max brushes his hands on his pants and then opens his arms. "Come on."

"I can walk shoeless." The vibe in the air is already awkward enough. He doesn't offer conversation this time and picks me straight up, cradling me to his chest. We walk back to the house in near-complete darkness. Judge follows. A near kiss averted—for now.

CHAPTER ELEVEN: OUT OF NOWHERE

Two weeks later, the rain has still not ceased. My boredom meter is at an all-time high, although I've started another painting again. This time the old barn is my inspiration. It's also been diverted by another movie-watching session at Max's and one more trip to his uncle's dancehall. We went when Collin and Emily made another trip to town. It was a blast, and we all had a great time. Collin apologized repeatedly for getting me drunk the last time, which was funny, seeing as he tried the stunt again. This time I knew better, however, and curtailed his attempts. Maybe it was too saint-like, but I avoided all alcohol, very much aware I had zero desire to puke—especially not in front of Max—even though he'd taken care of me without question the last time.

I pretend as though the near kiss didn't happen, and Max acts much the same. What's strange is that Max didn't go off to his mystery place this past weekend like he typically does. It was raining, and I speculate that that had something to do with it. I don't ask him about it, however.

After the phone call with Eric in College Station, I don't mention Max any longer. Despite my efforts in avoiding Max as a topic on calls with Eric, his mood teeters often when we're on the phone. To compound things, the calls are every other day now, and text messages between us are nearly non-existent. I glance at his photo or slip on his jersey to keep his memory fresh. It's not the same. I'm flustered, and anger builds daily towards his choice to go so far away. Or is it that I'm trying desperately to make something work that simply can't? I've given myself and my heart away, and now it hurts.

The rain stops on a Wednesday afternoon, and by Friday morning it is just dry enough for a run. I'm thrilled to get out again. I need to clear my head, figure out what I really want to do about Eric before beginning school next month.

After a quick breakfast, I grab my shoes from the foot of the stairs and lace them up. I tug down my black running shorts that have ridden up my thighs. Nicky walks into the room, carrying a basket of laundry, as I'm finishing up. She's in linen pants and the denim shirt she often wears when she paints. Evidence of former paint projects is displayed in random dry-splattered spots on it. She must have been painting this morning.

"Off for a run?"

"Yes, I need a good run," I answer.

"Okay. If we're not here when you get back, Pacey and I have to drive a few towns over. I need to meet with the builder. We're finalizing some things before they break ground next week."

The weather has been terrible, and other than the surveyors staking out the house's property line, the plans for starting the construction continue to get pushed back. Dad is busy at the clinic, so Nicky's been taking the reins on finalizing some things.

Pacey emerges from his room and squeezes by me to get down the last step.

"You could say excuse me, you know," I stare directly at him. Nicky is now in her bedroom and yells,

"Say 'excuse me' to your sister, Pacey."

"Yeah, yeah." He stares back at me. "Excuse me. Better?" he says in a high tone, as if mimicking me.

"Oh, whatever." I shake my head and push myself up from the step.

"Where is your Maxi-poo?" Pacey laughs and heads for the kitchen.

"He's a friend, and I don't know where he is today. Why don't you go ask him?"

Pacey doesn't reply and I don't care to get into it with him. There's no point.

I grab the iPod I brought down from my room and adjust the buds in my ears. Judge has been on his doggy bed in the living room. I call for him and he perks up.

I call again, "Let's go boy."

He stretches his front legs and then steps off the bed, following me out the front door. It creaks, in desperate need of some oil as it closes behind us.

After a good stretch of my arms and legs, I breathe a whiff of country air. It's still slightly damp from the recent rains, and the smell of nearby wet hay gives off a sweet scent. I actually like it. Sunshine on my face washes the gloom of the past rainy weeks away. It's going to be hot, and a thin layer of sweat has already accumulated on my arms and face. My bright-yellow running top creeps up slightly, exposing my belly button as Judge walks with me leash-less to the entrance of the property.

"Off we go." I look down at Judge.

We both take off at a good pace. I feel tension in my shoulders, no doubt from the recent stress of figuring out the male situation in my life. I shrug them, hoping they will loosen.

Yes, this run is exactly what I need. I run out my aggression, confusion, and everything in between. We pass Max's family's house, and continue on. Music through my ear buds drowns out everything around me. Wind is nonexistent in the still, hot air.

I stop a moment near a small creek, and Judge bee-lines for the water, submerging and splashing in it to cool off. Afterwards, he gulps down a few swallows of water and returns to meet me at the road. He halts in front of me and shakes his body. Water slings from his fur.

"Judge, stop," I giggle.

I feel water droplets hit my legs then Judge suddenly stills. Music is still blasting in my ears. It looks like Judge is growling, but I can't hear it. His teeth are showing and his hackles rise.

"What the—?" I turn down my iPod. "Judge?"

He doesn't respond to me in the slightest and continues to glower at me, or at something directly behind me. This aggression he's displaying has never happened before, and it terrifies me. I hear another growl, but it's not Judge's. Instead, it's coming from behind me. *Oh, no.*

I steadily turn my head to discover a nasty-looking, wiry-haired dog the size of Judge, ready to strike. His eyes have an evil quality to them, and there is foam dripping from his jowls. Alongside the wicked-looking dog are two others, just as gnarly and nasty-looking, but slightly smaller. Once is missing an eye, and the other has protruding ribs.

Oh, hell, what am I going to do? This was exactly what Max had warned me about. Time freezes as I fear what is about to unfold. What do I do? Do I run? What will they do to me, or worse, to Judge?

Judge creeps slowly past me and towards them. His face still looks ferocious, his teeth gleaming. I'm going to be sick. Adrenaline fires through my body like lightning, but the pace of everything around me feels as if it's moving achingly slow. It's the longest few seconds of my entire life.

"Judge, stop!" I yelp. It's no use. The dogs tangle into a mangled mess of fur and teeth. Judge is horribly outnumbered. I scream and cry out, but there is no one to hear me. I feel tears fall from my face. They cloud my vision. One of the dogs breaks free from the fight; the one missing an eye. It growls ferociously at me. My body finally hits autopilot. I flee towards Max's house.

I make out the sound of the dog's paws on the ground and hear pants of its ravenous breath behind me, but I sprint at unrivaled speed, full-out adrenaline pumping through my veins. I only have to make it to Max's house.

Run. Run.

I feel my iPod fall to the ground as I glance back a nanosecond. The mangy dog is several yards back but still racing towards me. I reach the entrance to the Baras' property. The gate is closed. *Shit.*

From a quick surveillance of my options, the barbed-wire fence is my only choice. I hit the ground and army crawl beneath it. I feel barbs pierce the skin on my back and legs, but I don't pay a lick of attention to it. The dog is nearing the gate. I jump up and resume my sprint, feeling liquid roll down my legs. I don't dare look back. *Almost there.*

"Max! Max!" I scream as loud as my tired lungs can manage.

I don't see anyone outside, but Max's truck is out front. *He's home. Someone's home.* It seems like unending distance to the front door. My eyes are so blurred by sweat and tears I can barely see. My legs want to give out. I reach the door and pound on it with all my might.

"Help! Help! Help!" I feel for a doorbell and hit it over and over.

It opens and I collapse on the entry floor. It's Mrs. Bara. She cradles me in her lap.

"Shut the door," I shriek. She doesn't hesitate a moment and slams it shut.

"Maxwell!" Mrs. Bara yells out. I wipe my eyes just as Max emerges.

"Oh, my God, Taylor! You're bleeding!"

"What?" I glance downward to observe blood running down my legs. "It doesn't matter. Please help. It's Judge. He's hurt." Max drops to the floor and takes me from his mother's arms. He wipes my tears with his thumbs.

"What happened?" Horror strikes his face.

"Dogs. Wild dogs," is all I can manage, beginning to cry harder. "Help him. Please," I struggle. "One of them— one of them followed me here." I'm out of breath and can't speak anymore.

Max presses me to his chest.

"I'll go get your father," I hear Mrs. Bara say as she runs off somewhere in the house.

"Where is he?" Max questions in my ear.

"Up the road. Maybe half a mile," I say, clamoring for a deep breath to stop the tears and gather my wits.

"Let's get you to the bathroom for those cuts. Then I'll go find him." I abruptly push away from him at the idea.

"No. We need to go right now. The cuts don't hurt. I left him—I left him there." Max examines me quickly with his eyes.

"Are you sure you're okay?" A look of grave worry is on his face.

"Yes." I struggle to stand. Max helps me up. A loud boom filters through the house from outside. Like a gunshot.

"It must be Dad," Max says.

Mrs. Bara resurfaces. "Your dad has gone looking for them. He must have found one of them. Honey, let me bandage these cuts." She reaches out towards me.

"She wants to go with me, Mom," Max responds for me.

"What?" Mrs. Bara says, confused.

"Oh, Mrs. Bara, thank you. But I have to find him. I need to find Judge," I whirl around, straight for the front door.

Max opens it and I run out to the truck, flinging myself in. He runs around to the driver's side, fires up the truck, and flies down the drive. He starts clicking on the gate opener.

"Come on. Open," Max curses under his breath. It finally juts open and he hits the accelerator.

"Which way?" Max asks.

"Left," I say. My heart begins thudding harder, frightened at what we may find.

I make out a brown canine figure in the middle of the road, not too far off. Max slams on the brakes in front of it. We bolt out of the truck.

"Oh no…no. No!" I shake my head and collapse near Judge's lifeless body. The other dogs are nowhere in sight. Max drops to the ground, lowering his head to Judge's stomach.

"I hear a heartbeat," he confirms loudly.

"Oh, Judge, boy. I'm so sorry." I rub the top of his head. No response. Blood drizzles down his sides and from his mouth. There is also a large gash on his front shoulder.

"Go to my truck, Taylor. I have an old shirt somewhere in the back seat. Grab it. Quick!" Max shouts.

"Okay." I scramble to the truck and rummage in the back seat for the t-shirt, locate it, then return to Max and Judge. "Here." I fling it into Max's hands and he firmly wraps the large gash on Judge's shoulder with it immediately.

"I've looked him over. I see a lot of gashes and bites, but we won't know more until we get him to the vet." Max tenderly touches the injured dog, scouring for other apparent injuries. "I'll carry him to the truck and set him in your lap."

"Okay. Let's go," I beg. Max scoops him gently into his arms. I dash for the truck, swing open the door, and clamber in. Max gingerly lays Judge in my lap. He whimpers. *A sign of life.* "Oh, sweet Judge. Hang in there, boy."

I hold the large lab in my lap, like a parent with a small child, and caress his ears and face with one hand while holding the ragged t-shirt bandage firmly in place with the other. Max rushes around the other side of the truck, jumps in and takes off at Mach speed for town. I don't want this to be my last moments with Judge. I can't lose him. Not like this.

CHAPTER TWELVE: PLEASE MAKE IT

I sit in the small office of the veterinary clinic in Schulenburg. Max is situated next to me in the waiting room. Blood has dried on my legs, and my tank top adheres to my skin from sweat and the cuts on my back. Mud is smeared on my stomach and shorts from when I slipped under the fence. I must look like I've been to war.

The only sound in the cold, fluorescent-bulb-lit room is a ticking clock on the wall. *Tick, tick, tick.*

I replay the sequence of events in its entirety like a movie reel in my head. *I abandoned Judge. But what if I had stayed? Could I really have done anything? He protected me. I can't think of enough kind acts in this world that I could ever do to make it up to my Judge... if he makes it.* My heart shatters into a thousand pieces with each passing second of uncertainty.

Max spoke briefly with his father while we were on our way here. Mr. Bara informed Max that he "took care" of the dog he'd found on the property, and would be on the lookout for the other two. Max then phoned my dad shortly after we arrived. I expected him any moment.

Max shifts in his orange plastic chair. It creaks, breaching the silence of the last several minutes.

"I have a first-aid kit in my truck. Let me clean up your cuts, Taylor." I don't answer. He drapes his arm softly around my shoulder and tenderly brushes it with his fingers. "Please," he begs softly.

"No," I breathe in deeply. "Not until I know he's okay."

Max doesn't prod further with the request. Instead, he pulls me to him and I rest my head on his shoulder, tired and worried. The tick of the clock resumes as the only sound in the office. I assume all staff on hand has gone back to work on Judge.

The door suddenly slams open.

"Oh, Taylor, honey. Are you okay?' Dad barrels in, still wearing his white physician coat. The quiet is gone.

"Dad." I rush up and dash into his arms.

"I'm so glad you're okay." He releases me from his embrace and steps back to look me over. "Wait, you have blood on you." He bends over and glances at the dried blood on my backside.

"I'm okay, Dad. I had to climb under a fence. It scraped me up, that's all," I reassure him.

"We need to get these cleaned up," Dad exclaims.

"No. I don't care about the stupid cuts. I just want to know if Judge is okay," I cry out, suddenly feeling weak and faint. "Whoa," I speak, stricken with a sudden bout of dizziness, my legs feeling like Jell-O.

"Sit down, Taylor," Dad scolds and guides me to the closest chair. "All the adrenaline's worn off, no doubt, and you're probably dehydrated."

"I'll go get some water, Mr. Sabian. I have some in my truck." Max rushes out the door. Dad sits down next to me and hugs me to him.

"We'll do everything we can, Taylor. I'll tell the vet to do whatever is necessary to save Judge." He releases me and looks into my eyes. "For now, take some deep breaths. You've been through a lot today, and your body is tired."

Max returns to the waiting room. "Here."

He unscrews the cap from a bottle of water and hands it to me. I take a sip. My mouth is parched, and the cool water running down my dry throat soothes it.

"Thank you." I look up at Max.

He gives a quick nod then sits down in another empty chair nearby. In less than a minute, he stands straight back up when the door from the back portion of the vet's office opens. Dr. Schmidt, the middle-aged vet in jeans and a denim button-up shirt who met us when we arrived with Judge, emerges.

"Is he okay?" I can't help myself and yell out.

"Hi, everyone," he says in a simple, monotone voice, giving away no hint of Judge's condition.

"Sir, I'm Dr. Sabian. Taylor's dad." Dad reaches to shake the doctor's hand. Dr. Schmidt reciprocates.

"Ah, yes; the new doctor in town, right?" Doctor Schmidt asks.

"Yes. How is he?" Dad responds just as calmly as the vet's welcome. Their calm demeanor must be an inherent practice in the medical world. I'm screaming inside for nothing more than an answer.

"I'm going to be honest with all of you. I am not sure if he'll make it through the night. We will most definitely need to keep him and keep a close watch on him. He lost a lot of blood, has a punctured lung, and we had to sew up

the gash on his front shoulder. He's in rough shape." His
expression is serious and honest.

I hear Dad converse back and forth with him, but it's
muffled to my ears. My mind dissolves into a foggy mess.
If I had thought I wanted to faint before, it's inevitable
now. All emotion, speech, and any remaining energy have
departed.

The world goes black.

***

"Can I do anything for her, Dad?"

"No, son, just let her rest. She needs rest more than
anything right now."

"Is he going to make it?"

"I know he'll try, son."

The conversation draws me from sleep. My eyes
flicker open and closed, adjusting to the light of a nearby
lamp. I slowly shift my head. I'm on the couch of our living
room.

"Ouch." Something is tender. My hand moves to the
source. My legs. My fingers slide delicately over large
Band-Aids on the back of them. I slowly sit up to observe
them more closely. When I do, my back is sore, as well.
Then the memory of the reason for the wounds returns. A

152

combined sigh and wince escapes my mouth. Slowly, I place my legs on the wood floor of the living room. I can tell it's dark outside through a nearby window.

"Taylor." Nicky walks into the living room with a startled look at seeing me up.

"What time is it?"

"It's almost nine," Nicky answers, walking over and sitting next to me on the couch. I recollect that the last time I saw her was earlier in the morning. She's in pajamas and a robe now. Her hair is still perfectly styled in her angled bob.

"You feel okay?" She rubs my shoulder lightly with her hand. "Thirsty or hungry?" Nicky asks.

It's just now I realize I haven't eaten all day, not since we returned from the vet's office. *I remember now*. I passed out, Dad helped me come to, and then we were able to see Judge, but only after I begged Dad and Max. They wanted to get me home. I remember. I remember seeing Judge. I held him so tenderly, kissed his soft head, and told him that I loved him. But I don't know if he heard me.

"Oh, poor Judge," I say aloud, recalling the moment.

"He's a fighter, and you know it, Taylor," Nicky reassures me and takes my hand in hers.

"What time did I go to sleep?" I ask her.

"Three o'clock; just after you took a shower and your dad doctored your cuts." She releases my hand and pushes up from the sofa.

"Why don't you come get a bite to eat? I made spaghetti earlier. I can heat some up," Nicky offers. I think on it a moment, but I really have no appetite.

"Thank you, but I think I'll just get a glass of water. Food just doesn't sound good right now," I respond and glance up at Nicky. Dad appears from the kitchen.

"I thought I heard talking in here." Dad walks to Nicky and looks down at me.

"Would you like any aspirin?" he asks.

"No, but thanks," I answer. Pacey comes out of the kitchen as well, racing up to me.

"Oh, I love you." He hugs me hard. I'm stunned by his offer of affection, and a bit frozen at the unexpected gesture. After a few seconds, I hug him back.

"Thanks, Pace."

He releases me. This may be a once in a lifetime moment to experience my little brother's sweet side.

"So, Dad says we can go see Judge tomorrow morning before we leave," Pacey says surprisingly.

"What? Leave for where?" Am I missing something?

"Your cousin April's wedding, in Houston," Dad answers and drapes his arm around Nicky. "Don't worry about going right now, Taylor. You can make up your mind in the morning. We'll only be gone one night, and we'll only leave if we get a good report from the vet."

"Oh. Okay." I'd completely forgotten. We'd gotten the invitation months ago, but I hadn't even thought of it, with all my recent life changes. The last thing I want to do right now is go to a wedding. But I'd worry about it later. There has been enough craziness for one day.

***

I finally get to my cell phone after all the day's dramatic events. Eric hasn't called. Why hasn't he called? I haven't spoken to him in two days.

All I want is to hear his voice right now. To listen to him tell me it will all be okay. To tell him all about Judge and what happened.

I think of how much I love Eric holding me. I love him comforting me. I love him. *Or do I love the memory of him?*

I sit on the edge of the bed, with a desperate desire to hear his tranquil voice. I dial his number and draw the phone to my ear. It rings. No answer, then voicemail. I call again. It rings and still no answer and voicemail.

"Why won't you answer?" It's almost eleven at night. I fiddle with the phone in my hands, contemplating my options. I decide to leave a voicemail and call him one last time. It rings and then,

"Hello?" a female voice answers. I can't speak. "Hello?" the voice asks again.

I hang up, stunned. Confused. Pissed! Who was it? Do I want to know?

I stare at the phone. The battery is almost dead. I power it off, wanting nothing to do with Eric should he call back.

"Jerk!" I'm burning mad. There may be an innocent explanation, but I'm still furious. It's been one hell of a day. All I needed was to talk to him. And now this? I am an emotional mess from all that's transpired, and the tears come quickly. I cry until there are no tears left.

CHAPTER THIRTEEN: WHAT IS THIS ABOUT?

The house is noiseless. My face is sticky from dried tears, and my back and legs are still tender but not painful. I am thirsty, achingly thirsty, and I have to pee. I shove the covers off and climb out of bed. Something outside the window catches my eye. Even if still half-asleep, I'd know the vehicle anywhere. Max's truck.

"Why is he here?" I yawn and rub my eyes.

I wonder about the time. Typically, I would grab my phone, but an unwelcomed recollection of the reason I turned it off last night slaps me in the face. Judge is all that matters right now, and I reject any other thoughts where Eric is concerned. *But I'm still pissed.*

I'm filled with a desire to leave for town straight away to find out Judge's condition. That is, if Dad or Nicky don't already know. I decide heading downstairs first is the best option. I'm decent in grey pajama shorts and a camisole. It'll do.

I will brave whatever awaits downstairs.

Rounding the base of the steps, the grandfather clock in the living room says it's eight-thirty in the morning. It's too quiet. Where is everyone? Inventorying each room downstairs, I don't see Max in the house either. I end the quick search at Dad and Nicky's room. The bed is made, with no signs of life. *Hmmm?*

I head for the bathroom, intending to ready myself quickly. My face is a nasty mess in the mirror. *Yuck.* Turning on the faucet, I drop my face to the water and cup some liquid into my mouth. A few swallows satisfy my immediate thirst, but I ache for more. First I pee and complete the tasks of washing my face, brushing my teeth and whipping my hair into a makeshift bun. I quickly dab gloss and a bit of makeup on, in case Max awaits somewhere. This will do, I reckon, then flip off the light and walk to the kitchen. After grabbing a bottle of water from the fridge, I suck it down. Boy, I'm thirsty. Now to figure out where everyone is.

I peek out the front door. Glancing over where Dad's truck is typically parked, I notice that it's gone.

"You're up." The sound of Max's voice frightens me. I gasp then step fully outside.

"You startled me." I place my hand to my chest.

He is sitting in a rocking chair, with one leg propped up on the opposite knee. Much out of character, he's in loose-fitting pants and a Texas A&M t-shirt, not spiffed up in his signature jeans and pearl-snap shirt. *Hmm.* He appears relaxed.

"How long have you been out here?" I'm curious.

Max stands.

"'Bout the time your parents left. Oh, half an hour ago or so," he answers, walking over to me. I raise my head as he nears, to meet his eyes.

"Since they left?" I recall Dad mentioning we would only go to Houston today if word were received that Judge was okay. A glimmer of hope lights within. But why would they go and not tell me? "They went to Houston?"

"Yes. The vet is a family friend. I called him bright and early at seven. Dr. Schmidt said Judge has a long way to go, but the outlook is promising."

"So he'll be okay?" I glimpse up at Max.

"It looks like he'll make it." Max grins, conjuring the release of all tension from the prior day's events. I step towards Max and place a hand over his heart.

"Thank you," I gaze at him.

"For what?" he appears confused.

"Just, thank you." There are too many things to thank him for; helping Judge, racing to the vet, calling the vet this morning. 'Thank you' sums it all up. I remove my hand, dropping it back to my side.

"Have you been waiting here just to tell me that?" Why would he? He could've just called.

"Yes and no." He runs a hand through his sun-kissed hair. "I have a surprise for you. I want to take you somewhere. I hope it will help lighten your spirits after yesterday." His exquisite features and the mention of a surprise have me entranced.

"Wait, it's Saturday," I suddenly realize. "You always leave on Saturdays. You're not going today? The weather's nice. You always say you can go when the weather is good." The sun already glimmers over the landscape, alluding to a magnificent day ahead.

Max reaches down, toying with my makeshift bun, and flashes a teasing grin. I swat his hand away.

"You're still not going to tell me what it is, are you?" I say, agitated but excited, crossing my arms in front of me.

"You'll see." He leans over and places his palms upon my shoulders. My body tenses.

"Do my parents know about this?" I'm desperate to know why they left without me if Judge is doing better. Not that I cared to go to the wedding, anyway, it's just that it's atypical. But again, everything since coming here has been atypical.

"Of course they do. I told them all about it. They said, and I quote, 'It's just what she needs'." His hands pull away from my shoulders. Goosebumps emerge, and I shiver.

"You know, they must really like you."

His lascivious smile returns. "You think so, huh?" He's either being clever, or enjoying my curiosity where my parents' reaction is concerned.

"I know so."

"Well, Miss I Know So, why don't you go get dressed?"

Crap, I'm still in my PJs. It's the second time now that this has happened. I blush, turning to go inside and change.

"Wait." Max's rugged hand touches my back. His fingers trace the outline of the bandages there. I catch my breath, absorbing the euphoric heat it ignites in my belly. "Do these hurt?"

I turn my head. "No. They're a little sore, but nothing I can't stand," I assure him.

"I need to make sure they're okay before we j—, go today," he quickly corrects.

"Almost gave it away." I laugh now, dying to know his plan. "I'll be right back."

I pull away and his hand falls.

"Just make sure to wear somethin' comfortable and some tennis shoes. We'll go see Judge before we leave, if you'd like," he instructs, then offers. I glimpse at him before heading inside.

"Yes. I want to go see him," I affirm.

Max's interest in caring for me, and even Judge yesterday, coupled with his astounding kindness, warms my heart despite our ability to rile each other's nerves to the point of frustration. He illuminates feelings within me that I can't explain. *What is this?*

***

Once we arrive at the vet's office in town, we are guided to a kennel in the back. It's quiet, with only a sprinkling of cats and dogs in a few other kennel cages.

"He's here," Dr. Schmidt announces. The kennel area is strewn with a padded dog bed and blanket. Judge is laid

162

out, looking comatose. His front leg is in some sort of a sling. "He is probably groggy from all of the medication. He's on quite a bit."

"Heavy painkillers?" Max inquires.

"Yes. And antibiotics," Dr. Schmidt answers.

"How long will he be in the sling?" Max continues.

"Definitely until the stitches come out," Dr. Schmidt returns.

I forget this is the world Max is embarking into at school, veterinary medicine. It's no wonder he's asking all the questions I wouldn't fathom.

"May I see him? Touch him?" My eyes prick from tears, but I'm relieved to be here with Judge in the flesh.

"Of course," Dr. Schmidt confirm.

I maneuver open the latched kennel area gate, step in and move slowly to Judge. I sit down and slide gradually to him, afraid of bumping him.

"Hi, Judge." I want to believe he hears me. Maybe he can. Pining for a sign of life, I stroke his ears. They're like velvet. I lean down and kiss his nose, observing that he's been washed of the bloody wounds I had seen yesterday. He remains motionless, except for the rise and fall of his chest. "We'll get you better, buddy. We will." I lean over

163

and kiss him again softly, moving my fingers over his back and surveying his wounds. He suffered so much at my expense.

"I'll give you a moment," Dr. Schmidt offers, and disappears.

Though a small area, Max maneuvers in, dropping next to us on the floor.

"He's a good dog, Taylor, a strong dog. We'll all help him back to health." Max pats Judge's frail body softly.

Judge's eyes open for a brief moment then close.

"Judge?" I place my hands around the battered pup's face. His eyes flicker open again and he releases a quick sigh, followed by a wince. His rough tongue licks one of my hands.

"Oh, sweetie." I lean down and kiss his head. Judge leans into my hand. His interaction may be minimal, but it's all I need, and it elicits optimism for his recovery.

CHAPTER FOURTEEN: TRUTH REVEALED

Where is he driving? We've been in the truck for over an hour and a half. All I know is we are headed west on Highway 21; not an area I know well.

"How long until we get there?" Wherever *there* is.

"Not much longer," is all he offers.

"Still not giving me a clue?" My mind is toying with ideas, but I can't gather anything concrete. Whatever he has in store is truly a surprise.

"No, ma'am," he grins naughtily then stupefies me with his next question, "Everything okay in the Eric department?"

I sit stunned as fury builds in me. My face feels hot from anger. It must be red.

"I don't want to talk about it," I utter hastily. The female voice on the phone still has me hot and bitter.

"Okay. Sorry," he apologizes.

"You don't need to be sorry, I just don't want to talk about it," I mutter. Opening up to Max about the issue will only make things worse. Besides, the day has turned into a positive, and only looks to get better. Drowning it with my childish rant over the Eric call would be a mistake, I reason. I change the subject. "Have you ever taken anyone to do whatever we're going to do?" I prod.

"Nope. Not a soul," he answers. I feel his eyes on me and I turn to meet them.

"Why now?" I ask with wonder.

"You're different."

My insides melt. *Different how?* "I don't know what I'm supposed to say…"

"Don't say anything," he answers. It only makes me appreciate him more. He doesn't push, yet a part of me wants him to push. I'm attracted to Max and jaded with Eric. Tides are definitely turning.

Max reaches for my hand, curling his fingers over my knuckles. He doesn't let go. I don't pull away. We stay that way a few minutes until Max announces,

"We're almost there."

I survey the surroundings. A lot of open land. No city or building in sight. We pull off onto a side road. There is a sign:

Crockets Skydiving

2 miles

"Skydiving!" I yelp, thrilled and instantly nervous. So, this explains the supposed body bag. It must have been a parachute or something.

"Yup. Skydivin'." He squeezes then releases my hand.

"Wait. I can't just jump out of a plane."

"Relax. You're not just jumpin' out of a plane all by your lonesome." He bursts out laughing. Then I remember he said he'd discussed this with Dad and Nicky.

"Wait, wait, wait, my parents agreed to this?" I ask and bury my head in my hands, nodding back and forth, excited but in disbelief. They'd never agree to this. Or would they?

"Without hesitation," he promptly affirms. "They said you were eighteen, and it's just what you needed right now."

"Excuse me? What parents have you been talking to?" I chuckle. Every hair on my arms stands on end. This is surreal. "How exactly does this work?" I question as he pulls into a parking lot adjoining a hangar-like building. An airstrip parallels us.

"Well, you'll be jumpin' with me; tandem." My heart leaps in my chest at the thought of being so close to him. And the fact that I will be freefalling through the air at who the hell knows what speed, trusting another human to assure I live through it excites me even more.

"And you've done this how many times?" I wonder just how safe this proposition truly is.

"Five hundred and eleven, after today." My mouth gapes open. "Wow," is all I manage.

"I'll get you up in the air and back down in one piece, Scout's honor." He holds up his fingers in a mock scout-salute, grinning from ear to ear.

"When did you learn how to do this?" I can't help but ask.

"Did it once when I was eighteen. Fell in love with it. Joined a club at school and never quit." Max astounds me. I never would have pegged him for the skydiving type—until now.

"Now, are you ready to go jump out of a perfectly-good airplane, or what?"

"Okay. I guess." My initial excitement is wearing off and the reality of what I'm about to do is sinking in.

"You'll do just fine. I won't let anythin' happen to you." I could pounce on him right now with the combination of feelings he's arousing in me. I'm reeling with excitement. Max is far beyond anything I ever expected this summer.

***

"I'll be hooked to you from behind, here." He presses his hand to the small of my back. I quiver. "Keep your knees bent and your head up."

We are inside the hangar facility. Several other people are here. First-timers I think, like myself. They're in some sort of a quick prep class. Max says we don't have to do it. He's showing me the ropes instead.

"Hey, Max. How's it been?" a middle-aged man with light brown hair tinged with gray shakes Max's hand.

"Great, Sam. Ready to jump today. I brought a friend." He raises his hand towards me. I step up. "Taylor, this is Mr. Crocket, the owner," Max concludes the introduction.

"Pleasure, Taylor. Jumped before?" Mr. Crocket asks.

"Oh, no; I've never skydived." I shake my head no.

"You're in for quite a treat," he chuckles.

169

"So I've been told." I peek over at Max, patting his arm. He reciprocates, draping his arm around my shoulder.

"We'll be taking this group up in thirty minutes or so," Mr. Crocket announces.

"Okay, thanks Sam," Max smiles appreciatively. They shake hands again.

"Nice to meet you, Taylor; have fun up there," Mr. Crocket sh   ny hand and walks away.

"So, where were we?" Max picks up where we left off, then informs me we will be jumping from 13,500 feet up. I can't gauge how high up that is. This is nuts. And then he tells me the type of plane we'll go up in, a DHC-6 Twin Otter something or other. It's not small, but a hell of a lot smaller than any commercial aircraft I've ever been on.

After the entire spiel, Max goes to the counter and picks out a jumpsuit and goggles for me. He returns with a gray-looking suit, but I see bright, hot pink ones behind the counter.

"Can I get a pink one?" I beg as soon as he places the frumpy gray thing in front of me.

"Yeah, fine; if ya want." He bunches up the gray suit, looking a bit annoyed. "Just go ask 'em for one in an extra small." He hands the gray one to me and I walk back to the counter.

"Can I get an extra-small pink jumpsuit?" I ask a young man with long wavy hair.

"Sure thing." He takes the gray one from me and plops the bright pink one in my hands.

I smile, happy to have something a little more fun to wear. I turn back to Max, who's already dr____ __ his black jumpsuit. His blond-flecked hair shimmers from the light of a nearby large window. He doesn't see me staring at him, so I drink him in. He's a delicious sight—tall and firm. I am about to attach myself to this gorgeous man and jump out of a plane. My heart is a damn mess. A gravitational pull sparks within me each moment our bodies are close, eliciting the desire for his body against mine. *Damn it, how can this be right? I love Eric. Don't I?*

I walk back over to him before he notices my ogling. "Alright, I got it." I hold it up.

"I'll have to remember that you like pink next time." *Next time?* This excites me. "Go ahead and get it on. We'll be out of here in about ten minutes."

I shuffle into the suit then raise the goggles to my forehead. I make a final check of my tennis shoes' laces and double-knot them. My hair is still plopped in a bun on top of my head from fixing it that morning.

The group assembles and heads outside.

"Here we go," Max grabs his gear.

My stomach is in knots. I breathe through my nose long and deep, and exhale long and slow.

"Taylor. You got this." He glows down at me with white teeth showing. My heart pangs in my chest from the surety in his glittering eyes.

"Okay," I want to sound confident but I'm so unsure of myself—about what I'm about to do, about Max.

Max wraps his arm around my waist and squeezes me to his side. My body naturally leans into him. He releases me and we walk out after the group has exited. It's a bright day, and the summer air is still.

"Damn, it's a great day for jumping," Max says and again reaches for me, lightly caressing my back over a bandaged area. I instinctively reach where his hand is. His face turns serious, "You're sure your back and legs don't hurt? You can still stay back if you want." This is it, the moment to back out.

"No, I'm fine. I want to do this." Decision time is over. I'm going to do something crazy. Everything about this summer has been crazy. It's my own personal moment to release all that has happened.

We are the last to board the plane. I count twenty heads after we take a seat as the plane taxis. The plane's engines roar, racing down the runway and up into the summer sky.

Max squeezes my knee as the plane ascends. I grab his hand and squeeze back—hard. My ears pop as we climb, so I wiggle my jaw. Eventually, we level off.

The group we boarded with is in tandem pairs, and they make their way towards the door. It opens and, pair by pair, they disappear into the sky.

"Okay, let's get ready!" Max yells over the loud engines. I adjust my goggles before we stand, his front attached to my back. I feel him mess with a few things connecting us. Then he leans down next to my ear. I can feel his hot breath. "Let's head to the door."

I walk slowly, bracing myself on anything possible as we shimmy to the door. We are the only ones still aboard, besides the pilot.

My body goes completely numb and butterflies are having a ball in my stomach, when the wide-open sky comes into view.

"Holy—Max, that's a long way down!" I scream. The wind whips hard around the opening.

"You can do this!" he yells back. It's so loud between the wind and the engines. "I'm going to count to three, then jump," he asserts.

"All…alright," I hesitate but agree.

"One, two—"

CHAPTER FIFTEEN: TIRED OF RESISTING

We freefall at an extraordinary speed. I feel air whip through every orifice and I see land far below us. It's so crazy and exhilarating all at once.

"You okay?" Max hollers and holds a thumb's-up in front of my face.

"Yes!" I scream back, offering a thumb's-up to confirm.

We spin and fall. Fall and spin. Everything that has happened is non-existent, and I absorb the sensation. I'm pressed to Max firmly, my legs bent over his. I could be seconds from death's door, but right now, all I feel is pure joy. I will never forget this.

Abruptly we catapult back up into the sky. I hear the parachute release. I'm startled and gasp.

"Wow." I soak in the scene all around as we float down to earth.

"Pretty cool, huh?" Max's lips graze my ear. My body tingles.

"Amazing. Simply amazing," I reiterate.

We float beneath the canopy. The scenery is breathtaking and it's quiet except for the sounds of Max maneuvering the chute with his hands.

All existence disappears. It's heavenly.

We cascade to the earth in silent company until we are a few hundred feet from the ground. Other jumpers are dotted around the drop zone.

"Just let me land. Lean into me and sit just like we talked about, okay?" he instructs as we near touching down.

"Got it," I nod.

His feet meet the grass and we travel quickly a few steps then fall softly backwards to the ground, my body on top of his.

"Now, how was that?"

"One of the best things I've ever done," I laugh. I'm elated with what's just been experienced. The parachute falls behind us as Max fiddles with the harnesses and clips. I slip the goggles off my head.

"Okay, you're free," he laughs.

I stand slowly, off-kilter. Max grabs my elbow to assist then removes his goggles. Once standing, I turn to him and leap into his arms.

"Thank you, Maxwell," I whisper into his ear.

"Anytime." Max grasps me tightly. His warmth radiates around me. After a moment, he loosens his grip and I slide down his body to the ground. His eyes meet mine. I am compelled to kiss him right here, right now. I bite my lip, nearly puncturing it as I resist my urges. I'm fighting a losing battle.

Just kiss him, Taylor.

Max sweeps his hands around my hair and cups my face. He leans over and kisses the top of my head. *This is not going to hold up much longer. The harlot within me is gaining speed, and Miss Goodie-Two-Shoes will eventually lose.*

"Let's go home," Max turns and begins wrapping the chute back up.

There goes yet another chance to kiss this mesmerizingly-handsome man. My libido is a hot mess.

***

The sky has changed as we drive home. Dark clouds roll in, erasing the beautiful sunny day.

"Ugh. Is it really going to rain again?" It's annoying.

"Looks like it." Max surveys the clouds out the driver side window. "You want to go see Judge one more time before I take you home?" Max offers. This guy thinks of everything.

"Yeah, I do," I confirm.

Max exits for Schulenburg and heads over to the vet's office.

***

Judge is still groggy and on the bed at the clinic, but I am grateful to have a few more minutes with him today. It's four forty-five in the afternoon, and Dr. Schmidt opened the clinic to let us in, only because Max called and asked. Thank goodness for his connections.

We leave for home and, in the peaceful silence, I start pondering the day that has just passed, surprised by the feelings surfacing for Max. But my thoughts are derailed by the brooding clouds overtaking the sky. Thunder rumbles, rattling the truck windows.

"This is going to be a nasty one," Max concludes.

"Looks pretty mean," I reiterate.

"Are your parents coming home tonight?" Max questions.

"I don't know; probably not. But I don't have my cell with me. It's at the house." I'm again reminded of the reason it's off. I push the thought away and release the bun on top of my head. My hair cascades down my shoulders and I run my fingers through it.

"Here, use my phone," Max reaches for his cell in the console and hands it to me. I call Dad's number. It rings and he picks up.

"Dad?"

"Taylor?"

"Yes, it's me," I confirm.

"Whose phone number is this?" Dad questions.

"Oh, sorry, it's Maxwell's. I don't have my phone with me."

"How was it?" Dad doesn't hesitate.

"Oh, my, gosh. It was amazing!" I gush.

"We hear Judge is looking better, too," Dad adds.

"Yes, he is. I saw him twice today."

"That's great to hear, hun," he sounds relieved.

"So, are ya'll heading home tonight?" I ask.

"No, we're staying with Nicky's sister. The wedding starts at six and it would be late driving back. We'll be home in the morning. Will you be okay?"

179

"No worries, Dad. I'll be fine." I give away nothing about the weather.

"Okay. Well, call us if you need anything."

"I will, Dad. Love you."

"You, too." I hang up and hand the phone back over to Max.

"They'll be home tomorrow?" Max asks.

"Yup."

"Want to stay at my house in one of the spare bedrooms?" Enticing, but I resist. A night at Max's puts me dead center of the lion's den for my desire to run rampant.

"No, I'll be fine. I'm a big girl." I muster courage. Truthfully, I hate the idea of staying home alone during a crazy storm. Here I go again, trying to be the saintly girlfriend for Eric.

Jerk is probably cheating on me anyway.

Lightning strikes a tree just off the road. I scream out loud.

"Taylor, I'll just stay at your house until this passes. Okay?"

"Alright," I relent. My shoulders shudder with my nerves in overdrive from the lightning strike.

We reach the farm a few minutes later. The tree branches whip violently and thunder booms. Max parks the truck as the angry sky releases its fury, dumping water in heavy buckets. We run to the house, soaked by the time we reach it. I scramble for the key under a flowerpot by the door. I find it and we dash inside.

"Some rain," I acknowledge.

"We better hunker down," Max instructs. "Why don't we see if anything about the weather is on the news?"

"Okay," I agree. I move to the living room and turn on the television. It's black with the message: no satellite.

"TV satellite's out."

"Bad weather will do that," Max affirms.

I flip on a lamp. The brooding clouds have wiped out the daylight. The rain hammers down on the roof. My tight cream tee is damp and water drips on the floor from my hair.

The mood in the room shifts at the realization that we are completely alone with nothing to do in the pouring rain. This is exactly what I had hoped to avoid.

"So—" I can't finish my sentence. A crack of lightning echoes from outside followed by a deafening boom of thunder. The lamp flickers out. We've lost power.

I catch my breath as my heart thumps in my chest. Max moves over to me and rests both of his hands on my shoulders, looking down at me. His thumbs stroke my skin and I finally exhale. His eyes penetrate mine.

"Hey, breathe. It's alright. Let's head over to my house. I'll bring you home after this passes. But why don't you bring some things just in case?"

"O-Ok," I stutter.

He glides his hands down my wet arms, which only increases the intensity of my heartbeat. I tear my eyes from his and walk upstairs carefully in the faint light. I gather a few things and stuff them into a small duffle bag. The rain has only worsened, pelting the roof, and I can barely see the yard outside the window. It has rained a lot lately, but not like this. This time it's more vicious. I return down stairs and Max is waiting for me, leaning against the front door. *God, he's so hot.*

"I'm ready." *In more ways than one.*

He takes the bag from my hands. "I'll carry this for you."

Max opens the door and lets me out first then I lock it after we step outside into the gloomy, wet weather. My hair blows from the moist breeze gusting beneath the porch roof. I feel my hands shake from both the damp chill in the air and my wavering nerves as I mull over what could happen tonight. Max grabs one of my hands. It's warm and firm against my clammy palm. "Good grief. Your hand is like ice, Taylor." He rubs my hand in his. "Everything is ok." He assures me. But I'm not sure if it's because of the weather or if he's sensing my yearning for something more. "Let's go." He tugs my hand in his and we run back into the rain pouring rampantly.

His hand doesn't leave mine as he guides me to his side of the truck, which is closest to the house. He pops the bag over the backseat then helps lift me into the truck, and I slide over as he jumps in and closes the door. Our clothes are soaked. Max turns over the ignition, flips on the lights and windshield wipers then carefully pulls away from the house, focused on the barely-visible road. The wipers whip back and forth but it's not enough to keep up with the torrent of water coming down. We are halfway to Max's house when the truck's lights reveal a river of water running across the road crossing Max had warned me of.

"Oh, boy," Max utters as he bears down on the truck's brakes. Water is racing over the road just feet in front of us, not to mention a giant tree limb is lodged smack in the middle of it.

"The water went up fast." I can't believe it.

"It's raining hard. It could be like this for a while. Plus, I can't pass with that branch stuck there."

I look over at Max, who's biting his lip. He looks back at me with intense eyes, and I don't think it's because of the crazy weather or our inability to cross the road. Whatever's been building between us is like a dam about to burst, and you could cut the sexual tension in the air with a knife.

"So let's go back to my house." I know it's the only option, and right now I just want to get there—fast, for more reasons that just getting out of the rain.

He releases his lip from his teeth. "Don't have much of a choice, do we?" He squeezes my thigh with one hand while the other rests on the steering wheel. His touch pulses through me and only leaves me wanting him to touch me in other places.

With great care, he backs the truck up and makes his way down the road the way we came. The rain is relentless as we pull back up to my house. Max reaches for my bag in the back of the truck.

"Let's get inside," I urge him.

He nods and we both pile out and sprint back to the house. But it's pretty pointless, as wet as we already are. After leaping to the porch, I unlock the door and open it quickly, allowing us an escape from the wild weather. Max dashes in behind me and drops the bag just inside the door, closing it behind him. His wet, brawny figure meanders towards me. My heart pounds, my body aching with desire. His gaze pierces through me, and I'm out of fight. Max grasps my head and pulls me straight to his lips, kissing me with such passion it leaves me lightheaded, defenseless. Our lips eventually part and I open my eyes. The flaming look in his eyes gives away his thirst for more. I want it, too.

Max's hand shifts and glides down my back. He pulls me to his firm body after reaching the small of my back. Ablaze with a frenzied lust, all that I've withheld from Max suddenly crumbles away. I wrap my hands tightly around his neck and then fist his hair. He meshes his lips again with mine. His tongue invades my mouth.

Max lifts me to him, and I wrap my legs around his sculpted waist. He walks forward, pressing me against a nearby wall. My back stings a moment from the cuts, but I ignore it. He winds his hands around the nape of my neck, softly peppering it with gentle kisses and intermittent grazes of his teeth. Arousal races through me. I want him so badly. Have I ever wanted anything this much?

Max traces his lips back upward to my face then kisses me deliciously once more and breaks away, "Are you okay? Do you want me to stop?" His eyes entrance me.

I shake my head. "No. Don't stop," I whisper.

He leans in, pressing his forehead to mine. "I want you," he compels. His hands gather around my waist. My legs are still firmly around him. I nuzzle his roughly-stubbled cheeks.

"Let's go upstairs," I urge.

He releases me achingly slowly. My feet meet the floor. His tongue ravishes mine again where we stand. Out of breath, I push him back and move a hand into his. He grips it tenderly and raises it to his lips. He teases it with feathery kisses, from fingers to shoulder. By the time he finishes, my body's blazing with want. I turn and guide him slowly up the stairs. We reach my bedroom and he stands behind me again, caressing my neck with his attentive lips. I reach for his neck behind me, urging him to continue. He does.

After he's through, he draws my back to his stomach and, with capable hands, feels the length of my body, chest to waist. He stops at the base of my shirt, pulling it over my head. It drops to the floor. He leans down, kissing the bandaged areas of my back. It's soothing.

I spin around and peel his shirt off, dropping it near mine, then pull his face down to me. His kiss is so addictive, it's like a narcotic—I need more. He undoes my shorts and slides them to the ground, lips still on mine. I follow suit with his pants.

He clutches me to him, his hands beneath my behind. My breasts press against his chest. We move to the bed and he lays me atop it—slowly. His body covers mine and he throbs against me. My body is filling with angst.

Despite my need, Max takes his time, learning my body, making me tremble with desire. He leaves me for a moment, and I whimper at the loss. I hear him pick up his pants from the floor, quickly followed by the crinkle and tear of plastic. Less than a heartbeat later, he returns to the bed, once again covering me with his comforting weight. He pushes into me slowly, and my body gradually accepts him. My body is on fire, wanting every part of him. My breasts press against his chest, hard and smooth above mine, as his hands rake through my hair and he kisses me wildly. He thrusts into me and my body complies, meeting his rhythm with passionate hunger for more. We make love. Not once, but twice. The storm rages on as every bit of my energy leaves in pure ecstasy.

CHAPTER SIXTEEN: UNSURE

I wake to crickets chirping outside. The moonlight peeks through clouds into my window. The rain must have stopped. Did I just dream that? I shift in bed, completely unaware of the time.

I sit up, naked beneath the sheets. There is a warm body next to me, keeping the covers tightly in place. Max. He's asleep with his hands tucked beneath a pillow.

Oh, my God. I'm not dreaming. I swipe my hand through my hair, no longer straight but wavy from getting wet in the rain earlier. A quick play of recent events dashes through my head.

Max stirs. "Taylor?" He reaches for me, gathering me to his chest. His body is naked and inviting.

"I'm here." I embrace his arm wrapping about me and caress it with my fingers.

I drift back to sleep.

***

189

The sun is blinding through the window. I have to cover my eyes. I sit up naked. *Oh, no. Mom and Dad could be home!* I bolt from bed and search for Dad's truck outside the window. It's not there. *Whew.*

I turn around. Max isn't here. *What?* I quickly search my dresser drawers for shorts and a shirt to throw on then hop down the stairs. I'm still glowing from the night's quixotic events.

I quickly tour downstairs. Nothing. *Huh.* I look out the front window. Max's truck is gone. My heart sinks. *Why would he leave without saying goodbye?* I move to the kitchen table, sinking into a chair. It feels cool against my skin. A note with unfamiliar penmanship rests on the table. I pick it up and read:

A breaker tripped. I've fixed it. Hope you slept well.
– Max

That was short. Last night was so amazing. I've never known passion like I experienced. My heart is full. Is this what real love is? I've never had this ravenous sensation enthrall me. Not even with Eric. *Shit, Eric.* I lose my breath.

My phone. It's been off this entire time. I race back upstairs, note in hand, and stub my toe in my rush. "Ow."

Once upstairs, I rub my foot then scavenge for my phone on the floor of my room. I find it and power it up. It's almost out of juice. I search for the charger and plug it in just as a series of several messages ping, one after the other. The first one:

Call me Taylor. Why haven't you answered?

The second one:

Are you ok? I've left 3 voicemails.

The third and original:

My roommate's girlfriend said the phone rang over and over so she answered, but no one was there. Are you ok?

Oh, no. No. Why did I falter so quickly? Was it really his roommate's girlfriend? Would it really have changed my choice last night? I sink to the floor and cradle my head in my hands. What to do? I want to cry. I want to laugh. I want to throw something and break it. What the hell have I gotten myself into? I can't just leave him hanging. I quickly send a text, knowing I'm nowhere near ready to talk.

I'm ok. Don't worry.

I'm just not ready to talk right now.

I hit send, hoping to curtail his concern for a while, and throw the phone back onto the floor.

191

I want to go see Judge. He'd make me feel better right now, but it's Sunday, and I don't have the contacts Max does. *Why did he leave?* I question again. Maybe he called, too. I grab the phone again, but there are no missed calls from Max. There are, however, eight from Eric. Eight!

I can't call. Not now. I am elated with all that I'm feeling, but it's masked with a layer of shame. I can't face it now. I decide that silence is best. I need to think, because this can't go on.

***

Nicky, Dad, and Pacey make it home at half past noon. I would never in a million years dream of telling them Max stayed over. Perhaps this is why his note was so frank; in case they saw it. It would give nothing away except that he had fixed a breaker and cared that I got a restful night of sleep. *Anything but restful. Amazing is more like it,* I reminisce. But they will never see the note. I've tucked it away in a drawer, under my socks.

Max does not surface, nor does he call. I feel abandoned after such a beautiful night together, but it's overshadowed by the conversation I know I need to have with Eric. *Should I really tell him? How will he react? Does it even matter if I feel something for Max? And I do.*

192

The entire Sabian brigade is full of questions about skydiving when we eat dinner together later in the evening. I put up a front.

"What was freefall like?" Nicky asks, intrigued.

"Fast, fun….crazy," I tell them, then spoon potatoes into my mouth.

"How high up do they take you?" Dad wonders.

"Um, 13,000 feet or something." I try to remember.

"Did anyone die?" Pacey jokes, and shifts his broccoli around on his plate in a clever attempt to make it look like he's eaten it.

"No, you nerd," I shake my head.

I hear my cell phone ring from upstairs with Eric's ringtone. I haven't answered his other attempts today. I'm not ready.

"Excuse me," I push away from the table and make my way upstairs. The phone stops ringing by the time I reach it. I sigh and bite my lip, wondering how to face this. I turn the phone off for now. The poor guy probably thinks terrible things. I feel downright evil. This is not right.

I need to sleep on this.

***

"Judge, I'm so confused," I confide to my canine friend. His tail thumps harder. I softly stroke my fingers through this chocolate fur. He rests his head on my lap.

He looks much better today. I drove to see him first thing after waking. I sit for nearly an hour with him, relieved he's improved, and sorting out my mess of a love life.

Moving here was supposed to be boring. It's been anything but.

CHAPTER SEVENTEEN: RESURFACE

At the dock, sun rains down on me. My olive skin is turning another shade darker. The warm baptism of light is exactly what I need, lying on a beach towel in a green bikini. I unbutton the top of my cutoff shorts to tan my stomach evenly while reading *Beautiful Disaster,* feeling like my precarious situation is just as the title implies.

I have repeated the events of the summer in my memory—from Eric's departure to the tryst with Max—so many times my head spins. It's late in the day and I make up my mind to call Eric tonight. I will face it; more than anything, he deserves to know. I'm not a liar, and I had never set out to cheat. The silence ends today, and I'll deal with whatever it brings. The only thing that's kept me relatively sane is painting. Almost finished with the barn piece, I feel like I've unlocked a piece of myself I'd forgotten. Dad insisted I not go running anymore without something to protect myself. He came home with an assortment of pepper sprays. A bit much, but I get it. He only wants to ensure that the nightmare with Judge never happens again. What Dad and Nicky have no clue about is what unfolded between Max and me while they were in Houston, and I pray to God they don't suspect.

I will drive over to see Max if he plays incognito much longer, too. I really wonder about his intentions now. I feel used. I sit up and scrunch into a ball as a large shadow casts over me. I peek up, setting the book down.

"Hey, Sprout," Max greets me, hands resting in his back jean pockets. His hair is covered with a ball cap. I can't see his face, staring up into the sun.

"Hey, yourself."

"Can I sit down?" Max asks.

"Sure." I roll my eyes. How is it the last time I saw this guy I was naked in bed with him, sated, and now I could chew him out?

"Are you alright?" He sits and leans back on his arms. His face looks confused.

"You haven't come by or called," I accuse and look away.

"It's not because I didn't want to," he affirms.

"What are you talking about?" I scrunch my shoulders. "I thought….I thought we had a beautiful moment. Moments, actually," I remind him.

"I didn't think you'd want to see me." He moves closer but still doesn't touch me.

"No; exactly the opposite, Maxwell." I'm upset, but could kiss the fool out of him.

"Does Eric know?" My heart stops.

How to answer that? *Think.* "No. Not yet. I haven't talked to him. At all." I drop my head, ashamed.

"Because you don't want to or because you don't have to?" he counters.

"What an arrogant thing to say," I raise my voice. "Did you come out here to school me on how *I* was the one in the wrong here? It takes two to tango," I remind him.

"No. I didn't mean it that way." His attitude shifts and he scoots towards me.

"I have so many emotions rolling through me right now, Maxwell. You were never a part of the plan, and now you're everywhere. Everything I think of. Everything I—" I have to stop myself, afraid I'm giving away too much.

Max reaches out and pulls me to him. I hug his neck. God, I love his arms around me.

I tip the bill of his hat up.

"So, why are you here now?" I wonder, gazing into his eyes.

"I couldn't stay away anymore," he alludes. "But you deserved time to think it through."

"Don't stay away," I beg, and caress his face. His unshaven skin tickles my fingers.

He leans into my hand.

"What do you want then?" he asks.

"You," I've said it. Now he knows. I feel the weight of my dilemma lift. *I love Max.*

Max's lips invade mine. Their euphoric effect takes over. The desire in me returns, as if it never left from the night we made love.

He shifts, taking me with him and pinning me beneath him on the beach towel. I feel his heart pound through his shirt. He buries his face in my neck. This is what I want. Him.

He moves his hand over my body, taking his time. We come up for air.

"Think we should go to the barn?" I ask.

"Perfect idea," he agrees and pushes himself up from atop me. He reaches down for my hands and pulls me up. I lean down to grab the towel and book then slip on my flip flops. He clasps my hand and we walk to the barn.

Luckily, no one seems to take an interest in the barn, except for me. I feel better thinking this, knowing what we are about to do, especially considering that Nicky and Pacey are home.

Max releases my hand as we approach and unlatches the door. The scent of familiar must and hay rushes out. We enter and Max closes the door. I drop everything in my hands to the ground.

My heart flutters and leaps, knowing what awaits me. I press myself against his rugged body. His arms envelop me. I crave his hands over every part of me. I push away just enough to undo the buttons of his shirt. I sweep it off his shoulders then move to his jeans, teasing him a second with my hand before unbuttoning them. He groans then yanks down my cutoff shorts. I'm left only in the bikini.

He leaves me a moment, grabs the towel and lays it hastily on bales of hay, then returns. I leap up into his arms and he spins around, setting me on the towel-topped bale. Sensual kisses follow, leaving me breathless.

He tugs my bottoms down. I follow, pulling his pants down. They fall to the ground. Before he steps out of them,

199

he shuffles for a condom and I hear the now-familiar tear. Then he slips it on. He hovers above me a moment, then slides inside me. I let him ravish me as we make love yet again.

CHAPTER EIGHTEEN: WHAT NOW?

"That was amazing!" I manage. My heart is pounding from the exhaustion of incredible love-making. Max rests on top of me.

"Yes, it was." Max grins and kisses my forehead.

"I could get used to this," I giggle, catching my breath.

"Me, too," Max says out of breath. He stills above me, his gaze consuming mine.

What I say next I don't expect to say, but I blurt it out without second-guessing myself.

"I love you." No taking it back now.

Max breaks his gaze from mine. My heart stops. He is too quiet.

"Max?" I search his eyes. He moves over.

"Taylor, I—" he doesn't finish.

I'm embarrassed and my heart is breaking. I push myself up and search for my suit and shorts, dressing quickly.

"Taylor, it's just… I told you I don't even know what love is. I thought I did," he explains.

"You are truly a jerk of the highest degree!" I scream, too sick inside to look at him.

He reaches for my shoulders.

"Don't touch me, Max," I spin around to break his grasp. "You used me for your own satisfaction, knowing damn well and good there was someone else in my life. I was willing to give that all up for you." Tears fill my eyes as my words spill out.

"Taylor, I want to be with you," he begs again, reaching for me. I wiggle loose.

"Yeah, so you can screw me. That's about the gist of it." I throw my hands into the air. "I can't look at you anymore." I plow past him and storm out through the unlatched barn door. I don't know where my shoes are and run barefoot to the house. Feeling dirty and used, and knowing I've cheated on Eric, I don't want to be near Max.

I can't stay in this forsaken place. I have to breathe. Get away.

"Taylor, stop," I hear Max behind me. I peek back. He jogs with his shirt half-buttoned, tugging his jeans over his boots.

"Leave me alone, Max!" I scream back, rubbing my thumbs beneath my eyes on my tear-soaked face.

I rush onward, somewhat relieved to see the house. Max maintains a distance as I make my way for the porch. Luckily, neither Nicky nor Pacey is outside to witness this. I swivel and rub one of my tired, dirtied bare feet as Max approaches.

"I don't want to leave, Taylor." Max's face is distraught. *Well, it's too late for making up now, asshole.*

"I don't care." I fist my hands at my side and feel my face red with heat. "I want you to leave, Max! Go!" I point to the truck, tears streaming from my eyes. He reaches for me. I back away, ready to kick him square in the goods with rage. He takes the hint and gives up, backing away then walking off. With drooped shoulders, he gets in the truck and drives off.

I bolt for the front door and fly upstairs to my room, sobbing.

"Taylor," Nicky's voice comes from downstairs.

"What?" I cry back.

"What is going on?"

"I don't want to talk right now." I slam the bedroom door and collapse on my bed, burying my face in the pillow. A light knock at the door follows.

"Taylor, can I come in?" Nicky requests. I lift my head.

"Fine," I yield. She opens the door.

"Good grief, Taylor, your feet are all muddy and you're crying. What on earth happened?" She flips my hair behind my shoulders then hugs me to her. It's comforting.

"I don't know what to do. My heart hurts." How much more do I really want to reveal? I wipe my eyes.

"Did Max hurt you?" I sit back up.

"No. Well, not physically, if that that's what you're asking." She takes one of my hands and squeezes it gently.

"You love him, don't you?" I look at her aghast; speechless.

"You do," she concludes.

"It's so wrong. There is Eric to consider and—" I am worked up, having to catch my breath. "I told Maxwell I love him."

"And?" Nicky's face contorts.

"He didn't say anything." I drop my head.

"I see," Nicky says.

"I just want to get out of here. I think I should go see Eric. I need to see him and face him. I don't want to hash out what we need to talk about over the phone."

"Taylor, I'm not so sure that's—" she's interrupted by Dad calling out as the front door opens downstairs.

"I'm home!" Dad announces.

"Let's talk with your father, okay?" She shifts off the bed and leaves my room. I desperately want a shower, and then intend to pack my stuff and get the hell out of Dodge. No matter what Dad and Nicky think, I don't want to be here if Max comes back, and I suspect he will.

I grab a clean pair of jeans, a blue V-neck tee, a bra and some underwear then dart straight for the downstairs bathroom. I race into the shower and clean off quickly. As soon as I've finished, I towel off and slip into my clothes. I glance into the mirror and notice that my eyes are swollen.

Someone knocks on the door.

"Taylor?" Dad sounds concerned.

"Dad, please, not now." *I don't want to talk now, people.* I rummage for the toiletries I'll need, cupping them in my arms and trying to open the knob with my elbow. It doesn't work. I place some of the items back on the counter. Now I can open it. I re-gather my stuff.

"What are you doing?" Dad asks.

"Leaving," I speak frankly.

"To do what? Go where?" Dad looks upset and confused. He's dressed in slacks and a dress shirt from work.

"I don't expect you to understand, Dad. I have money left from graduation. I'll drive to the airport in Houston and get a roundtrip ticket to Kansas City." I don't await his response, and climb the stairs with my arms full. It's a balancing act.

"Wait, young lady." He's mad. Or worried. Dad follows me up. "Does he even know you're coming?" Dad continues.

"Not yet." I don't glance at him as I yank a small travel suitcase from under my bed, hell-bent on getting out of here.

"Now, wait just a minute, Taylor–"

I spin around when he says my name.

"Dad, Maxwell doesn't love me and I've cheated on Eric." *Holy hell, did I just blurt that out to my father?* I blush. "I need to tell him everything to his face. I need to know if there is anything worth salvaging," I explain as my eyes blur with tears. I break away from his glance.

I grab clothes from drawers and stuff them into the suitcase. I shouldn't need much. I search for my graduation cash stashed under my mattress. Six hundred or so dollars. I stuff it in my purse on the dresser. Finishing, I zip the suitcase shut and grab the purse.

"Wait." Dad walks to me, reaching in his back pocket. He pulls out his billfold. "Here." He removes a credit card and several twenties. "Take this with you."

I look up at him. "What?"

"Three days tops," he firmly states. "And don't go to Houston. Go to Austin instead; it's a bit closer and the airport is easier to get in and out of." He hands me the money and credit card then returns the billfold to his pants pocket.

"Dad?" My eyebrows furrow.

"Yes, sweetie." He relaxes slightly.

"Thank you." I smile up at him. He reaches for me, embracing me in a hug. I inhale his aftershave; his signature scent I remember from childhood. He releases me. I step back.

"Love can be a tricky beast. There isn't always a clear black and white, but in the end, the heart guides you where you need to be." Dad's eyes are sincere as he adoringly rubs my shoulders.

He's such a good man, and exactly the type of guy I should be seeking to love and be loved by. Now to figure out if this awaits me in Kansas or if it's too far gone to save.

I quickly flip through flight options on my phone after Dad goes downstairs. The first flight to Kansas City is at six a.m. So, six a.m. it will be.

CHAPTER NINETEEN: DECISIONS

I hit call on the cell phone and get voicemail. I thought for certain he'd pick up. I leave a message.

"Eric. It's me. I can't explain a lot right now but I'm on my way there. I found a flight that should arrive at the Kansas City Airport at nine thirty-five a.m. My flight leaves Austin at six a.m. Please be there. Please."

I hang up the phone. What if he doesn't show? He probably has practice. *Why didn't I think? Geez.*

It's dead silent the rest of the night. Eric doesn't call back. Should I even go? *Yes, Taylor, you have to. You owe it to him.* I argue with my heart.

Max attempts to call five times. I am sick of it. I'm sick of him. I send it to voicemail with each try.

Whether Eric or Max calls from this point forward, I will ignore them both. It's time to let fate play its cards and take technology out of the equation. Truth be told, I'd rather not know if Eric will show up or not. I turn the phone off at 11 p.m. Besides, I'll have to leave the house at three a.m. to make my flight.

***

Beep. Beep. Beep. Beep. The alarm clock on the bedside table wakens me. It's crazy early and achingly quiet outside. I haven't slept a wink, in anticipation of the day ahead. There was no point to the alarm.

I drag myself from bed. Nervous, anxious… sick inside.

I get ready and gather my suitcase. Dad has been posted up in the kitchen, sipping coffee for half an hour as I prepare to leave. He goes to work in only a few hours.

He kisses me on my head as I depart into the dark pre-dawn.

"You be safe, baby girl," Dad requests.

"Always, Dad," I affirm then leave for the airport in Austin.

It's not an area I'm used to driving in, and it's dark. I trust the Mustang's navigation, eventually reaching the airport. It's lifeless. I park in a nearby lot, taking the shuttle to the terminal, and find my gate. I'm one of the first to arrive, avoiding baggage check. My bag is small enough to board with me as a carry-on.

I sit at the gate, my phone still off, and play out scenarios in my head. In the end, it all boils down to two choices: He either shows up or he doesn't.

I haven't seen Eric's pristine blue eyes in nearly two months. What will happen when I do see him, stare into his beautiful eyes, and confess that I've been unfaithful? If I were him, I'd be livid. But do I really know the entire story of what's happened since he got to school? Was it really his roommate's girlfriend the other night?

So many questions. Ugh. *Relax, Sabian. One thing at time.*

"Now boarding for Southwest, direct flight to Kansas City," is announced over the intercom.

This is it, the point of no return. I board the plane.

Here goes nothing.

***

I watch the sunrise through the airplane window. The flight is half-filled, so I had my pick of seats. The pilot announces ten minutes to landing, and my heart responds, thundering violently in my chest. I have to catch my breath as the plane begins its descent.

I haven't been on a plane in nearly two years. The last time was a family trip to Florida. Here I am, alone, heading

211

to a destination completely foreign to me. This is no family vacation. The answer my heart seeks waits when I disembark this plane.

We near the ground and I see the runway ahead, lights zooming down its sides. I can't think anymore. We touch down and I jolt slightly in my seat. *Not so bad.*

The plane taxis to the gate and the flight attendant announces the sequence of departures once we stop. I don't pay attention.

After situating at the gate, the plane door opens and I clamber over to the overhead bin to gather my luggage then roll it behind me off the plane. My stomach growls, but there is absolutely no way I could eat. I take my time entering the terminal. Everything around me fades away. There is only one face I'm seeking as I move to the escalator. It cascades slowly to the first floor of the airport. My head surveys the area on the way down. *Is he here?* I don't see him. My courage disintegrates.

I pull the carry-on behind me from baggage claim to baggage claim for thirty minutes. Nothing. I fear the worst. He won't show.

I stop and sit on my luggage, crushed. I have to get my bearings and figure out how to get home.

"Taylor?" I hear my name yelled in the airport full of strangers. My head looks all around. "Taylor!" I hear again. My heart stops. It's Eric. He's running in my direction in a Kansas State shirt and jeans. His dark hair has gotten longer by a few inches since he left. I can't move. My body trembles.

He reaches me, halting a foot in front of me. I break my stance and reach for his neck. I thank the Heaven above when he hugs me back. He's gained more muscle since I last saw him, too. I feel tiny in his sculpted arms.

"Hi," I whisper, grazing his ear.

"Are you okay?" he immediately asks, still holding me. He smells like the cologne I bought him last Christmas. I inhale a whiff of him and it takes me back to a different time; a time before all of this mess.

He pulls back, studying my eyes. His eyes are still as beautiful as I remember. I search them for something, anything resembling the love I thought I remembered. *Why can't I feel anything?*

"Thank you so much for meeting me here," I break the ice.

"Of course; I know you wouldn't fly all the way up here unless it was important." He smiles and strums my bottom lip with this thumb once. It tickles. *Can I really do this?* My legs feel weak as I hesitate in what I'm about to unveil. My knees give out and I collapse into his arms.

"Whoa," he manages, catching me. "Taylor. Take a breath." He strokes his hand through my long hair.

"I'm…I'm so sorry, Eric," is all I'm able to get out.

"What do you mean?" He releases my hair and pulls back, his dark eyebrows furrowing.

"I've done something."

He responds by releasing me completely.

"Wait." He holds up a hand. I halt any further commentary. "I don't want to know," he contends.

"What?" This isn't at all what I expected.

"It's better if you don't say it, Taylor. I don't want to hear what I think you're about to say." He is quite calm.

"I had to come see you. Face you. See what you still feel for me. If anything," I admit. He surprises me by stepping forward and taking my cheeks in his hands.

"Whatever happened with… him, it doesn't matter now." *He does know.* He pauses, and I'm entranced. "The truth is, I think we both got ahead of ourselves, thinking we could make this work. I wanted it to. It's just not reality, Taylor." *Am I really hearing this?* "I've met someone, too," he confesses. The weight of guilt vacates my body, yet my stomach turns at what he's just announced.

"You have?" I close my eyes and breathe until my lungs are full. My eyes reopen. "It wasn't your roommate's girlfriend on the phone, was it?" I ask anxiously.

"No, it *was,* actually. I was out with—"

"Her," I finish. He nods, confirming it all.

"So why did you meet me here, Eric?" His hands leave my cheeks and shift to my elbows when I ask.

"The same reason you're standing here now. It was only right to tell you in person."

"What now?" I wonder, and move my arms to the inside of his arms so they rest atop his.

"We say our goodbyes," he affirms. I feel strangely okay with this. No heaviness lingers on my heart in any capacity.

"Okay, then," I concur. He bends down to my forehead and his lips press against it. I squeeze his arms. His lips depart.

"Why don't I stay with you until you can get a flight home?" he offers.

"No. I'm okay, Eric." He cocks his head then shakes it.

"No, I should stay," he asserts.

"I'm a big girl, Eric. I can find my way home. Promise." I smile at him, looking at him from the other side of a relationship. I'm empowered and restored of spirit; except for what to do about Max when I get back.

"Okay," he relents. "Be safe, and don't let anyone break your heart, Taylor. I'm always here if you need me. I mean it." I'm thankful for his encouraging words.

He leans over one last time, kissing me like I'm a delicate flower. It's truly goodbye.

***

I rush to the airport bathroom, tears flowing. He's gone. It's really over. I'm relieved, but it still hurts. The person I gave my innocence to. I can never get it back, and he's taking a piece of me with him now that he's gone.

I lean over a sink and wash my face, imagining it can wash away the pain. It's useless. *What am I going to do now?*

***

I've been in this airport for nine non-ending hours, only able to change my return ticket to a flight later in the evening. Now is simply a waiting game, with nothing but time to think.

My conscience is completely clear where Eric's concerned. I feel free, in a sense. But Max's inability to confess any sort of love for me is still a crushing blow.

I will just go to school a completely-single woman, free of any attachment. It's not so terrible, I guess.

I've turned my phone back on to confirm with Dad and Nicky that I've made it. They seem relieved. I tell them about the decision Eric and I have come to. They agree.

Like a puzzle piece in its rightful place, I feel that Eric is a closed door. Now I just want to get back to Texas.

I set the phone in my lap, exhausted from lack of sleep, and ready to nap. It rings. Max's number. Am I ready to talk to him? I struggle with my gut saying yes and my head saying no. After the fifth ring, I relinquish the chattering in my head and follow my gut.

"Yes," I say shortly.

"Can I see you?" A yearning in his voice is instantly evident.

"I don't think that's really possible right now. I'm in Kansas City." I am still, frankly, unsure of myself.

"I know," he answers. "I'm here." My stomach cramps and my head is dizzy hearing that he's here.

"Wait. What? Where?" I look all around me in every direction. I'm in the boarding area. He couldn't get in here without a ticket.

"Downstairs by the baggage claim." That explains why I can't see him. I stand. My feet tingle from sitting so long. I wiggle them to regain feeling and pull the bag behind me toward the escalator back down to the baggage claim area, conversing with him as I walk.

"Why are you here?" I question. Not sure if I should be livid or flattered.

"I had to see you. I drove all day," he sounds distressed.

"What?" My heart flitters and flutters. I approach the escalator and scan the faces as I ride downstairs, just as I'd done for Eric earlier. But this time is different in every stretch of the imagination. I spot him, pearl-snap shirt, jeans, boots, and tousled dirty-blond hair.

"I see you," I verify. He spots me, too, and walks to the base of the escalator. I hang up the phone. He does, too.

I step off the escalator and he offers me his hand. I instinctively take it.

"I'm mad at you, you know?" I can't help myself.

"Taylor, am I too—" I know where he's going with this.

"Late?" I finish. I bite my lip. His eyes make my insides melt like butter. I don't know if I want this. I release my lip. "No." I soften.

His face relaxes and a smile takes over.

"You drove all the way here for me?"

"Ten hours," he answers. He looks tired.

"Why?" I don't understand why he'd go to all this trouble.

"I talked with your father this morning. I told him why I needed to see you and he told me exactly where to go." I'm aflame with wonder at the gesture. I look at the ground. My heart thuds so much I hear it in my ears.

"What if I had been here with Eric? Then what would you have done?" I lift my head back up at him. His eyes don't waver from me. It's pretty bold to drive all the way here, not knowing what he'd find.

"I had to know either way." He steps up to me and I'm forced to raise my chin to see his face.

"Either way, what, Maxwell?" I ask.

Max answers fast and firm, "I love you."

I lose my breath.

"What?" He caresses my face when I question him.

"I love you with everything I am." He leans down and kisses me hard and fast. I don't have a chance. I'm lost in him instantly. He enfolds me in his arms. My feet leave the ground. Bliss wipes away any doubts.

Eventually, our lips part, and he stares me square in the eye. "I'm so sorry. I should've told you right away. I was a coward. I knew I loved you; I just haven't felt what you make me feel before. I kept waiting for some sort of real confirmation so I would know if it was love. I—"

"Stop, Max." I place a finger over his lips. "It doesn't matter," I assure him. "I love you, too." I smile wildly with carefree joy.

He kisses me again, holding me even tighter to him. He's what I want. What I need.

We come up for air several minutes later. Max sets me down gently on the floor. He's giddy and glowing. I can only assume that I look the same way.

"Can I ask you a question?"

"Anything," Max affirms.

"When did you really fall for me?" I raise my eyebrows and grab his hand. He raises it to his lips kissing it softly.

"The day I first saw you on the road, running. No one's ever made me turn my head like that before." His answer consumes my heart. I believe him, because it was the same moment I fell for him.

Epilogue

The pond ripples from a nearby dragonfly gliding atop it. I glide my toe through the water, leaning back on my arms. I'm relieved that finals are over and I'll be graduating next month from A&M. I can't believe four years ago—to this day—Max told me that he loved me for the first time. We had cancelled my ticket and stayed the night in Kansas City, since it had been too late to drive. We made love that night, more times than I can count, and nothing's been the same since. I came to Schulenburg years ago, unaware that my world would be turned upside down. I thought I knew love, but I truly didn't until Max. Even more, he pushed me to pursue a degree in art. Nicky was, of course, thrilled. I would ed it without his encouragement. ..y core.

We've spent the last few years immersed in college and each other. Max will conclude his vet program soon, and then assist Dr. Schmidt at the vet clinic in town. Dr. Schmidt is looking to move to Victoria, and hopes to turn the practice over to Max eventually.

Judge fought through his injuries all those years ago, though he never fully healed. He's walked with a limp ever since, but he's still the same tenacious, loving lab despite that. He's never faltered in affection and loyalty toward me. During my frequent visits home to visit Dad and Nicky and the Baras, he's always elated to see me. I will never have another dog in my life like him. He's too special.

I feel hands sneak up behind me as I rest on the dock. Max.

"What are you thinking about?" Max slides behind me and dangles his own feet in the water on top of mine.

"Us," I giggle. He kisses my neck, making me shiver. "Don't start something you can't finish," I joke.

"Oh, I will." His lips travel to my ear. "I have a question for you."

"What is that?" I blush from the effect his lips have upon my ear.

He places a box with a stunning diamond ring in front of me.

"Marry me?" he asks. Just like when he first told me he loved me, I lose my breath. I, of course, answer,

"Yes."

Acknowledgments

I have so many people to thank on this project.
First of all, Barbara, thank you for the tremendous
opportunity to publish with Waldorf Publishing. I can't
express how much I appreciate your guidance, expertise,
and attention to detail. I'm incredibly thankful to you.

Chell Olson, you are an amazing editor and I can't say
thank you enough for your time and thoroughness on
Diverted Heart.

Lori Ryan, you are an amazing author and to have you
write my foreword was an incredible honor.

d Holli, as well as my mother,
ough the process was crucial and
your belief in me means the world.

To my amazing author critique group, you rock! Thank you
for assisting with the development of my characters and
suggestions which created an entirely new path for this
story than I'd originally intended. You made it so much
better!

Finally, to my family, I can only say thank you, thank you, thank you for putting up with my late-night writing sessions, enduring leftovers and sandwiches, and dealing with the occasionally frazzled mom/wife. You've shown nothing but love and patience through it all and supported me when I needed it most. I love you.

Author Bio

Beth Ann Is a wife, mother, blogger and book lover from Texas. Her passion is writing stories that draw a reader into a world where they can become the characters and experience a gamut of emotions. When she's not writing, Beth Ann loves to be home with her family and their two yellow labs. In addition Beth Ann is a sucker for super sappy romance movies, loves trying out Texas wines, an avid hot tea drinker and loves to check items off of her ever-growing bucket list.

A Communications graduate of Texas A&M University and active in the corporate world, in 2010 Beth Ann began writing as a bucket list dream and discovered writing to be her true calling. She hasn't looked back since and has numerous projects on the horizon.

Diverted Heart is a novel Beth Ann has greatly looked forward to releasing and has another novel, Fate's Betrayal to be released Fall 2015.

Website: www.BethAnnStifflemire.com

Blog: http://www.thewritingtexan.com

Twitter: @BASAuthor

Facebook:www.facebook.com/BAStifflemire

Pinterest:@BethStifflemire